tripped up

Neurospicy Book Club
Book Four

allie lasky

one

. . .

Elsy

"IT'S NOT THAT BAD," Bex says, glancing around.

Not that bad?

Totes clutter every corner, stacked in daunting towers. And the maze of unopened boxes is a definite fire hazard.

Sighing, I stare up at the ceiling. The last thing I need is to trip over one of these endless cardboard death traps and break my neck—or worse, my hands.

Bex and I met in grad school at Stanford, keeping in touch over the years, and when I accepted the Boston Symphony contract two years ago, it made sense for me to move in with her and her roommate, Vanessa. She had an extra room. I needed a place to stay. It was perfect.

The three of us became a tightly knit trio in our short time together. I'm going to miss them. A lot. I feel bad for leaving, even though I know it's the right thing for me.

When things went south for me in Boston, I knew I had to get out, and fast. A few weeks later, I packed up all my things and drove a moving truck across the country.

Austin will be a fresh start—one I desperately need.

A knock raps on my door, sparking my curiosity. The property manager already came by, and considering I don't know anybody else, I'm not expecting anyone. Maybe it's a friendly neighbor? Swinging the door open, I keep my fingers crossed that they're my age and single.

A tall, built, light-haired man stands on my doorstep. Wyatt Whitney, professional hockey player and the bane of my existence, props an arm on the doorframe and scowls.

"Elsabeth."

"What are you doing here?" I snap.

He arches an eyebrow. "That's how you thank me?"

A bitter laugh rips from my throat. "Thank you for what?"

"I invited him over," Bex calls from behind me. "Come on in, Wy."

I glare at her. "Why's he here?"

"Because you have ten thousand boxes and I want to get you unpacked sometime before next year," she says with a grin. "By the time I board that plane tomorrow, I want to be confident you're not going to starve or break your neck getting tripped up over the mess."

Only then do I see Wyatt's holding a toolbox, a bag of takeout in his other hand.

It's not my best friend's fault that I hate her brother. She doesn't know I slept with him—long before I knew they were related.

It *is* his fault that he doesn't remember we hooked up. He's always treated me like I'm nothing more than the scum on his shoes.

And yeah, I know it was only ever supposed to be a one-night stand, but for him not to remember me after?

My best friend Mitch invited me to go watch him in Ottawa for the World Juniors Championship, then took me to a bar to hang out with his hockey buddies. Wyatt came up and flirted with me, obviously trying to steal me away from Mitch. It's never been like that with us; we've always been strictly platonic, but Wyatt didn't know that.

He was cute; I was drunk and lonely, so I went back to his

hotel room with him. I snuck out in the morning before he woke up and was prepared to move on with my life. It was a great night, sure. But he was a hotshot hockey player at a college halfway across the country. The last thing I expected was for us to fall madly in love and have a happy ever after at nineteen years old.

But then I saw him in the hotel lobby with a few of the other hockey players. They were teasing him about going home with a "tubby butterface with good tits."

Hey, I was drunk, Wyatt said. *At least she put out.*

My stomach sank. The sweet, charming guy I'd seen glimpses of turned out to be a pig in his natural environment. What a disappointment. He was exactly like every other guy I'd met.

Our eyes met.

He saw my face.

He *knew* I heard.

And I've never been able to forget that.

I met Bex several years later in grad school, and it was another year and a half before I had a reason to meet her brother.

And when we met up in that dirty college dive bar, it was clear from the blank look on his face that he didn't remember me. He introduced himself with a disinterested handshake and immediately started hitting on another woman.

Since then, he's always treated me like any of Bex's other friends. Distant. Sometimes cold. Never cruel. It's clear he has no idea why I dislike him, but he's always given it back just as good, so evidently it doesn't bother him.

Wyatt sets the bag of takeout on the counter. "What do you want first, building furniture or lunch?"

"Lunch. Definitely," Bex answers for us.

My stomach lurches, and it's not from hunger. I hate eating in front of him. Over the years, we've only shared a few meals together, and always with his sister chaperoning. It makes me remember the sick feeling in my stomach that morning after we hooked up. I'm fat. I know I'm fat. I don't need it pointed out to me. Especially *after* a man had me naked in his bed.

Eating in front of him? That's a level of vulnerability I've never been able to get over. Almost as big as taking my shirt off in front of a man.

The apartment has a high counter with a bar area, but I don't have stools yet, so we stand around the peninsula. Even though I didn't bring much furniture with me, I have enough *stuff* to clutter the place. It sets my teeth on edge and pricks at my skin like a million bee stings.

That reminds me; I need to take my meds. Fishing the bottle out of my purse, I take deep, calming breaths, then tap a tablet into my palm and wash it down with a gulp of Coke. The carbonation makes it not the most pleasant experience, but one I'm well used to. Water is for the weak.

Bex grabs the bag of food, handing me the tuna salad sandwich and giving Wyatt two turkey clubs, keeping the roast beef for herself. She must have told him tuna salad is my favorite. Everyone else hates it, which means more for me. There's even a container of potato salad. Score!

"This place is right around the corner," Wyatt says.

I arch an eyebrow. Why is he talking to me?

"I snagged their menu in case you want to order from them again." He practically unhinges his jaw and shoves a club triangle into his mouth.

"I'm surprised you didn't get pizza," Bex says. "That's the classic moving food."

"Eliza doesn't like pizza."

The hairs on the back of my neck prickle. I hate when he calls me pet names. But also—

"And exactly *how* do you know I don't like pizza?"

I mean, I don't. Red sauce is so not my thing, and it

always gives me heartburn. Pepperoni is great, though—on its own, or in a sandwich, or even on a salad.

Wyatt shrugs again. "You've mentioned it."

"No, I haven't." Because people usually make fun of me or tell me it's impossible that I don't like it. I haven't had a good one. I haven't tried it enough. It's like sex. When it's good, it's good. When it's bad… it's still sex, so it can't be all bad. Right?

Sadly, like pizza for me, sex has always been bad.

Including sex with this asshat.

Well—the actual time we were in bed was fine. Decent. Above average. It's what happened afterward that's ruined my opinion.

"Sure you have," he insists.

My eyes narrow. "When have we ever had pizza together?" I don't know why I'm pushing this. It's weird that he knows this about me when most people don't. Hell, I don't think Bex even realized I don't eat it. Usually, we order Thai or Mexican.

Past tense. *Ordered.* Because we won't be living together anymore.

Blowing out a breath, I pick at my sandwich, my appetite evaporating at the reminder. Even though I've moved criss-cross the country on multiple occasions, this one is hitting the hardest. I loved my life in Boston. I have a large network of friends there, good friends. I have a job I loved.

Had.

Before things with Stephen got so tense it bled over into work, my life in Massachusetts was perfect. It was my favorite of all the places I've ever lived. I was promoted to the symphony's first fucking violin chair before I turned thirty. Now, at thirty-two, I was being tapped for major solos, and my music teaching gig was thriving.

And because my ex is an insecure asshole, I now have none of that.

Well, I'll still have my friends, even if our friendship has to be nurtured from a distance.

Luckily, the Austin Symphony wanted me. They even gave me a raise over what Boston was paying me, and with the lower cost of living, I'll finally be able to save a little. They liked me, just not enough to pay moving expenses, and even bootstrapping most of it myself, it hasn't been cheap. Plus, now I'll have to buy a car. I didn't need one back in Boston, but here in Texas, everything is driving distance.

Wyatt shakes his head, drawing my attention back to him. He always has to be the center of the fucking universe. His strawberry-blond hair is a little longer than usual. There are red flecks in his light scruff, and I bet if he grew it out, it would be red.

Why the fuck does he have to be so fucking hot? It's like the universe is taunting me, reminding me that the pretty people have everything, and everyone else—the fat, the ugly, the boring—has nothing.

I have nothing.

"Fuck. I have to buy a car," I announce, and Bex winces.

"Have you figured out what you want yet?" he asks.

"No. I figured I'd go to a used lot and find whatever's cheap and reliable."

If Mitch were here, he'd be able to talk the car salesperson into giving me a deal. As it is, shopping as a single woman, I'm sure they'll try to upsell and overcharge me on everything.

Wyatt makes a face, his disdain clear as day. "Want me to go with you?"

A frown twists my lips. "Why?" He doesn't like me—why does he want to willingly spend more time with me?

He shrugs. "Moral support?"

"Seriously?" I laugh, and when he doesn't crack a smile, mine falls. "You're serious?"

"I have some free time tomorrow after I drop Bex at the airport."

"You'd do that for me?" I've never hidden my dislike of him, and even if he doesn't know why, he's never backed down from a fight.

And we fight. Constantly.

"You're my little sister's friend. Sure." The distaste on his face sings another tune.

"Don't act like I'm twisting your arm."

Bex looks between us. "This is perfect. You'll look out for her, won't you, Wy?"

He grunts.

"I don't need anyone to look out for me. I'm fine." Crossing my arms over my chest, I nearly knock over my Coke can.

Quick as lightning, Wyatt's hand darts out and stabilizes it before it upends. He raises a brow, triumphant.

"Thanks," I mutter, rolling my eyes. So he has good reflexes. Whatever. He's a professional athlete. It's part of the job description.

"You'll invite her out, right?" Bex pushes. "I don't want her hiding away because she doesn't know anyone in town."

"I'll be fine. I've done this before," I remind her.

"Yeah, but it's different. With everything with you-know-who…"

My face pinches at the mention of my ex. "I won't be a hermit." Not any more than usual. I'm an introvert and a homebody by nature. "I've already got a lead on a book club and I'm sure I'll make friends at work. Besides, I have to get some teaching gigs lined up. I'll be too busy to go out much."

Bex laughs and pats my arm. "Yeah. Okay. Keep telling yourself that." She turns to her brother. "Make sure she doesn't bury herself in work, too."

Wyatt rolls his eyes. "She can take care of herself."

Yes! That's exactly what I've been saying.

Wait. Is he saying that because he doesn't want to help?

Not that I want him to. I don't need it—from him, or from anyone else.

Bex glares at him.

"Fine," Wyatt sighs. "I'll invite her to hang out."

Great. Now he's talking about me like I'm not even here. I don't know what's worse, the infantilization or his ignoring my presence.

He throws his to-go container into a bag and reaches for mine. His eyebrows dart up when he sees I haven't eaten my sandwich.

"Was tuna the wrong choice?"

I shake my head. "It's fine. I guess I'm not hungry."

Tilting his head, Wyatt hums. "I'll put it in the fridge. You can eat it later."

That's... surprisingly thoughtful.

Damn it. Why does he have to be anything other than the two-dimensional caricature of a villain I like to remember him as?

He deals with the trash, then lifts his toolbox.

"What do I need to build?"

two

. . .

Wyatt

ELSY ALEXANDER WILL BE the death of me.

It's been thirteen years since our night together. That's all we got: one night.

And then the next morning, I opened my big, fat mouth and ruined everything, and she's never forgiven me.

Hell, I've never forgiven myself.

I wasn't expecting her to pop up in my sister's life a few years ago, but they've been thick as thieves since they were in grad school, so I haven't been able to avoid her as much as I'd like. Living in a different city helped.

But then Philly traded me to Austin, and now Elsy's moved here, too, and I…

I'm well and truly screwed.

The only consolation is that her best friend, Nick Mitchell, isn't on this team. We faced New Orleans in the finals last season before Philadelphia eventually edged them out to win the Cup., adding to his list of reasons to hate me. He's never forgiven me for messing around with Elsy.

We were in Ottawa for World Juniors and he brought her along to the bar. He and I were vying for a spot on the first line, and one of our teammates dared me to win his girl out from under him.

She came willingly. And fuck, did she come. Multiple times—on my fingers, on my tongue, and later, with my cock buried deep inside her. She was breathtaking.

But then the guys were joshing me around the next morning and I said something I shouldn't have. I knew it the moment it came out. My mom brought me up to respect women, and I definitely would knock out anyone who talked about her the way I talked about Elsy.

So I guess it wasn't a surprise when Mitchell punched me in the face. The asshole broke my nose. And I know I deserved it, that and more, but in the decade since everything happened, he's gone out of his way to target me. He won't let it go.

And let's be honest, I needle him back. It gives me a high like none other. I'm a brawler by nature, and I never back down from a fight. Fuck, half the time, I start them. I finish them, too.

The two of us on one team? The league wouldn't survive it. It's bad enough we're in the same division.

As much as I regret volunteering to take her car shopping, I know Bex wants me to look out for her, and the last thing either of us wants is for her to be swindled by some smooth-talking car salesman. She's too sweet, too pure. She doesn't see the bad in anyone.

Except me.

As I pull up outside her apartment building, Elsy and Bex are waiting at the curb with a small suitcase. I pop the trunk and Bex stows her luggage before getting into the back seat.

"Are you expecting me to chauffeur you around?" I tease my sister as Elsy gets in the front.

"I get carsick," the blond beauty says. Her voice is quiet, but cold. "Is that a problem?"

"Not at all. Do you need a bag?"

The smell of jasmine tickles my nose when she shakes her head. Instantly, it takes me back to that night, her scent on my pillow comforting me long after she was gone.

"I brought my own. I'm usually fine as long as I sit in the front and don't read or play on my phone."

"Okay. Let me know if there's anything I can do to help." I increase the air conditioning on her side of the car. The cool air always helps when I'm feeling nauseous.

And fuck, the mere sight of her in my front seat makes me queasy. She's wearing a simple blue sundress that flutters around her thighs. A hint of white lace peeks out before she settles her dress around her.

Is she wearing a garter? *Fuck.* Elsy wearing nothing but garters and little lace panties… My cock throbs and I cough to clear my throat.

No. It wouldn't be that. Her legs are bare. She's not wearing stockings for the garters to hook to. And it's much too low on her legs to be her panties. So what is it?

The glimpse of lace taunts me as we drive across town to the airport. The late-September humidity slams into me when I step out of the car to grab Bex's suitcase and give my sister a hug.

"Take care of yourself," I tell her gruffly, swallowing down any emotion.

She laughs and rolls her eyes. "I'm almost thirty. I'm a grown fucking adult."

"Yeah, well, you're still my baby sister."

Bex pokes me in the ribs, which makes me twitch.

"Stop it," I hiss, batting her hand away. She knows all my ticklish spots and abuses them frequently.

"Take care of Elsy," she says. "She could use some support right now."

With a nod, I glance over my shoulder at the woman who has my dick in a chokehold. "I will."

"And hey," she whispers. "Maybe she'll warm up to you."

"Go get on your plane, Rebecca Lynn," I tell her, playfully shoving her.

She doesn't go inside the airport, though. She turns to Elsy and wraps her in a hug, whispering in her ear.

Elsy's mouth is pinched into a frown, her eyes downcast as Bex talks to her. As she nods, her blond ponytail sways in the wind. My sister says something that makes her giggle and Elsy wipes at her eyes.

"I'm going to miss you," Elsy says.

"I'll come visit whenever I can," Bex promises. "And we'll FaceTime, like, all the time. You'll barely even miss me."

Elsy's lip trembles. It takes everything in me not to shove my sister aside and wrap her into a hug until she never wants to cry again. I hate that she's hurting. And I hate that my trying to comfort her will only make her feel worse.

"I don't want you to go," she whispers, her voice raw. "Everyone leaves. I—"

Bex curses under her breath and hugs her again. "Oh, sweetie."

Elsy lets out a sob and buries her face in Bex's shoulder. "I'm sorry. You need to go. I'll be fine. I'll get through it."

"I can see if I can switch my flight…"

Setting a hand on my sister's shoulder, I ease her back. "I've got her," I tell her.

And then I wrap my arm around Elsy, curling her into my torso. To my surprise, she winds her arms around my waist and buries her face in my chest. My hand roves over her upper back, trying to soothe her.

"It'll be okay." I don't know which one of them I'm saying it to. Maybe even to myself.

Elsy's cries twist my stomach. I wish I could wipe away her tears and tell her everything will be fine. That she'll be stronger for having done this.

But I can't lie to her. I don't know what brought her to

Austin, just that the move was unexpected and not exactly her choice.

We're in the same boat. I've only been in town a few weeks. Training camp starts up next week. In my nine years in the league, I was lucky to make it so long without being traded. Once I made it out of the minors, I spent all of my time with Philly.

And then in the wake of our Cup win, they got rid of me. Traded.

Yeah, I'm not bitter, not at all.

Maybe this is what we need to have a fresh start—the both of us.

Bex's smile can't hide her sadness. Our relationship is stronger from living in different cities, but saying goodbye is always difficult. "I'll see you around," she promises, before she grabs her suitcase and wheels it up the ramp into the airport.

Elsy chokes out a sob and then releases me, stepping back. Black smudges beneath her eyes as she wipes them with the back of her hand. They immediately well with tears again.

"It'll be okay," I tell her.

Her withering glare could turn a lesser man to stone. As it is, my cock hardens in my athletic shorts at the derision on her face.

This is so wrong.

"Let's get this over with," she snaps, climbing back into the car.

I give myself a discreet adjustment before rounding the hood and sliding into the driver's seat.

"Have you thought about which dealer you want to check out?" I ask as I pull into traffic.

Elsy shrugs. "Wherever. It's not like I'm going to fall in love with the first car I see."

Spoiler alert: That is *exactly* what happens.

"I love it," she declares once we step onto the lot.

And just like that, the salesman approaches.

The small SUV is only three years old, a lease return from a nonsmoker, and has never been in an accident. It's a dark blue color with a light interior.

"I'm sure we can get you a good deal," he says, but his eyes are on me. He leers like he can see into my pockets—and my bank account. Just because hockey has earned me millions doesn't mean I'm about to spend all my cash. I've got to think about my future, for a life after hockey.

"Oh, we're just looking," I say casually.

Elsy opens her mouth, but I pull her into me, my arm draped around her shoulders again.

"Aren't we, pookie?"

She glares daggers at me.

"This one is great for new families," the salesman says. "When are you due?"

She smiles sweetly at him. "Not pregnant. Just fat."

His mouth gapes and his face goes purple. It's clear he doesn't know what to do.

"Um—I, um…"

"Why don't you run along and find your manager," I suggest with a hard edge to my voice. It's not a suggestions, and he knows it.

Her calm demeanor in the face of his rudeness only serves to piss me off further. She shouldn't have to be *nice* when people are assholes.

"Yes. I'll be right back," he says, before he runs away like a demonic hellhound is chasing after him.

Hey, I'm mostly bark, but he is right—I will bite. If the circumstances require it.

Elsy shoves me off of her. "I can handle it."

"He was an asshole."

"I know. But I can take care of myself." She crosses her arms over her chest, and my eyes flick down involuntarily before I force myself to meet her glare. "Don't be a creep, Wyatt."

"Sorry," I mutter, keeping my gaze on her face. "They're great tits."

"I know they are," she snaps. "Doesn't mean you get to look at them."

Or touch them, or suck on them, or fuck my cock between them. Trust me, I've fantasized about it more than a few times over the last thirteen years. I'm a disgusting, depraved pig. I don't need her to remind me. I remind myself often enough.

Another salesperson approaches. He's wearing a boxy, off-the-rack suit, his dark hair slicked back to cover the receding hairline.

"Can I help you?" he asks. He directs his question to Elsy, who glances at me out of the corner of her eye before giving him her full attention. She knows what she wants. The only thing holding her back is her own anxiety.

"I want this one."

"Certainly. Would you like to test drive it?" He focuses on her, but there's nothing sleazy in his gaze.

"Yes. Please," Elsy says. To my surprise, she reaches for my hand. "You'll come with me, right?"

Swallowing around the lump in my throat, I nod. "If you want me to."

The salesman—his name tag says Joey—heads off to fetch the keys.

"He seems decent," I comment, forcing my tone to stay casual. I don't want to bring attention to the fact she's still holding my hand. I almost expected her to drop it the second he was out of sight.

"At least he didn't stare at my tits," she mutters.

"Sorry."

She rolls her eyes. "I'm sure you are."

I am, but not for the reason she thinks.

I'm so fucking sorry for what I said. I have no excuses; I

was a young, insecure guy who thought I'd get in tight with the popular crowd.

Words have meaning. They have power and they can cause hurt, real hurt. Even back then, I knew that. Yet I said it anyway.

I'll never forgive myself for hurting her. And I'll do everything in my power to make it up to her, to show her I've changed, that I'm not the asshole she thinks I am.

I just hope it'll be enough.

three

. . .

Elsy

JOEY GIVES me a good deal on the car, and Wyatt talks him into a maintenance deal at minimal cost, so now I don't even have to think about getting regular checkups done. My wallet screams as I sign on the dotted line, but the fact remains, I need a car to get around out here. There's no bus route that will get me across town to the rehearsal space and back to the symphony for performances without major headaches.

Wyatt lingers even after I've finished signing the paperwork. Joey sticks a big red bow on the hood of the car and Wyatt snaps a few pictures on my phone so I can send them to Bex and Vanessa.

Now I have to go back to my apartment and unpack my seventy million boxes. Joy.

"D'you want to grab a drink?" Wyatt asks.

My eyebrows jump up. "Excuse me?"

He clears his throat, his face pink from being in the sun all afternoon. "A few of the guys are getting together. Super low-key."

Eyes narrowing, I try to figure out what his end game is.

"If you want to go home to your empty apartment, be my

guest," he says. "But I thought you might like some socializing with someone other than me."

I sigh. I would. I don't want to be alone. Even being around *him* is better than being by myself right now.

"Fine. Text me the address."

He nods, pulling out his phone and sending me the location details. My phone buzzes in my purse. O'Malley's Pub is only a few minutes' drive from my apartment. Joey already set up the Bluetooth, so I can punch a button on the screen and pull up the map.

As I slide into the car, my dress rides up, and I hurriedly pull at the hem before my lacy bike shorts are visible. The last thing I want is Wyatt seeing them—or worse, asking why I need to wear shorts under every dress and skirt.

Because my thighs rub together when I walk. Chub rub is no joke.

The bar is warm and welcoming. Instant hockey dude-bro vibes, but not in a bad way. It reminds me of the pubs in Boston and the dive bar I frequented in college. Old world sense of style, punctuated by signed hockey jerseys on the wall. Everything is decked out in navy blue and gold—the Austin Aces colors.

Because my best friend plays in the NHL, I keep tabs on what's going on in the league. I'm not a big fan of hockey, but I am a big fan of Mitch, so I try to show an interest in his career. Just like he's not actually invested in whatever piece I'm rehearsing, yet he shows interest because he cares about me.

Wyatt lingers in the pub's entrance. Almost like he's... waiting for me? But that can't be true; he'd never be so considerate as that. "The guys are over there," he says, nodding to the corner. Like I wouldn't recognize a group of tall, wide, and gorgeous hockey players. Come on. It's not like they're Clark Kent; everyone can see they're superheroes in hockey jerseys, even in their street-clothes disguises.

"Hey, man," one of them says, nodding to Wyatt. "Didn't think you'd show up."

Wyatt grunts like a caveman. If he wants to make friends with his teammates, he'll have to try harder. "Had things to do."

A hockey player with a wiry build looks me over. No way he's of legal drinking age. "Who's the chick?"

My eyes narrow. "Excuse me?"

Wyatt's hearty laugh makes my stomach turn. "This is Elsy. She's my kid sister's friend and just moved to town." He raises his brows. "That's Riley. Try not to eviscerate him. He's only a rookie."

"Welcome to Austin," says a guy with dark hair and a beard. "I'm Samson." He's wearing a wedding band and looks relatively normal.

"Nice to meet you."

"Cian O'Leary," says the man with collar-length hair, a neat beard, and green eyes.

And of course, I recognize Jack Vignier. Viggy is one of the older guys in the league—broadly built, dark hair, dark scruff. The kind of guy I'd like to take me home and do terrible things to my body.

Alas, he works out with Mitch in the offseason, so he's thoroughly off-limits. My best friend would kill me.

"Hey, Viggy." I give him an upward nod and get a rare hint of a smile from him in return.

This gets me raised eyebrows from the rest of the group.

"What's the story here?" Cian says, glancing between us, then back to Wyatt.

"Her friend is in the league," Wyatt says. "She's a groupie."

"Fuck off. I'm not a groupie." I roll my eyes. "My best friend is Nick Mitchell. He's with New Orleans."

"So what are you doing here with us, then?" Samson asks.

I shrug. "My job brought me here. I have a life outside of him."

Viggy snorts. "Does he know that?"

"Sometimes he forgets." I smile sweetly, even as I glare daggers at Wyatt. "It just means I have to remind him. Repeatedly."

The rest of the guys look around, evidently confused. I'm upending their dynamic.

"Now, as much as I love hockey players, and by love I mean tolerate," I continue. "Who do I have to talk to in order to get a drink around here?"

A waitress approaches at that moment. A worn plastic name tag proclaims her name to be Tina. She has the haggard look in her eye of someone on a double shift from hell. Light pop music plays from the restaurant's speakers, the volume low enough to render the lyrics indistinct. The scent of fried food lingers heavily in the air, making my stomach rumble.

"You want a drink?" Tina sets down three trays of wings in the center of the table.

"Yes, please. Tito's and Sprite. Thank you."

She gives me a tired smile. A little politeness goes a long way. "You got it. Any food?"

Even though I'm starving, my stomach twists at the idea of eating in front of all these guys. Strangers. *Men.*

"Oh, I'm fine. Thanks."

Wyatt, sitting across the table from me, raises his eyebrows. "You haven't eaten anything all day."

Who the hell does he think he is, chiding me like a child? I scowl at him, my lip curling petulantly.

"Get her a cheeseburger with fries and a side of barbecue sauce," he tells the waitress. "No tomatoes or ketchup, everything else on it is fine. Thank you."

Crossing my arms over my chest, I glare daggers at him. "Fuck off, Wyatt."

He rolls his eyes. "I don't want my sister to yell at me because I let you waste away."

Viggy pushes the basket of wings closer. "He's right. And Mitch would kill us."

"You're the worst," I mutter as I take one. I don't even like wings. They're too much work for not enough reward. If I'm going to suck on a bone until it's clean, I want it to be worth it.

The waitress brings me my drink and I give her a supportive smile. I've done my fair share of shifts bartending and cater waitering. It's how I put myself through grad school.

The guys talk around me, but I don't feel ignored. They're about to start training camp next week, while I'm about to start rehearsals.

It's the start of something new. I almost want to break into song, but life isn't *High School Musical*, and even if it were, I can't sing. Despite a voice practicum being a requirement for my degree, I'm a talented musician… who can't sing.

After a few minutes, my cheeseburger arrives, and I dig in. I didn't realize how hungry I was until Wyatt pointed it out. Which sours my appetite, sure. I won't let him hold me back, though.

I've been there, done that. Nobody can hold me down. Not for long.

———

My stomach churns as I walk into the rehearsal space. First days are as exciting as they are nausea inducing.

The Austin Symphony wants me. They reviewed my application materials and flew me out for an audition. They *hired* me.

Now I have to prove they didn't make an enormous mistake.

Lawrence, the musical director, is a sprightly man in his early seventies with a full head of frizzy white hair that practically screams *eccentric musician*. He was one of my professors at Stanford and my first mentor. When he moved to Austin a few years ago, he tried to recruit me, but I was happy in my position. Now that I need a fresh start, he was my first call.

The symphony salary isn't enough to pay all my bills, but once I supplement it with a few private music lessons, I should be comfortable enough. I just have to go out and meet people.

My least favorite thing to do.

Lawrence introduces me to Hilary, who gives me a quick tour of the facility and a rundown of the season.

Today's rehearsal is for the first fall performance. It'll take a lot of work to get up to speed on their repertoire, but I'm confident I can handle it. This is what I've been studying and training my whole life to do.

Anastasia O'Connor is the first chair violinist. She'll be my primary competition for solos; I was the first chair back in Boston, and I won't let myself stay stagnant in the number two chair for very long. We met briefly during my audition, and as I walk into the rehearsal studio, she gives me a tight-lipped smile.

"You made it," she says. I can't tell if she's talking about the job here or my arrival today. "There's a kerfuffle in the brass section."

"Oh?" I always like to be informed. It's not gossip if it impacts the job... or so I rationalize.

"I'm not exactly sure what's going on," she admits. "Something about a tuba player being asked to leave."

"I'll keep my ears open."

She nods, passing over today's music. The sheets are hole-punched already, so I can stick it into my three-ring notebook.

I'm familiar with the first piece we're doing, but not the second or the third.

"Are you settled in?"

"Mostly. There's so much to unpack. You'd think moving would get easier the more I do it." I shake my head with a resigned sigh. I have so much to do.

Staying out with Wyatt and his teammates was definitely the wrong call. They kept refilling my drink until I had too much to drive. Wyatt drove me home, and when I woke up this morning, ready to call an Uber back to the pub, my car was magically in my parking space in the apartment's garage. One of his teammates probably took care of it. They seem like decent guys—for being hockey players, which isn't saying much.

Lawrence begins rehearsal with a quick pep talk before launching into the day's itinerary. I catch a few people sending me confused looks, no doubt wondering who I am. With an eighty-member orchestra, there are a lot of musicians who come and go. They rarely come in as second chair, though.

As we wrap up, I notice Anastasia is quick to put her violin away.

"Do you want to grab coffee?" I ask, tempering my hopeful tone. I don't want to scare her off. We may compete for performance time, but we still have to work together.

She makes a face, and I can't decide if she's annoyed or disappointed. She's hard to read, but I'm determined to win her over. "Can't today. Got some things to do."

"Oh. Okay. Not a problem."

Guess I'll go back to my apartment and keep unpacking.

"I can do dinner after my errands, though," she says. Internally, I do a little dance. She's not brushing me off. Maybe she will be my friend and more than a colleague, after all. "Does that work?"

"Perfect." Am I coming on too eager?

She tells me the name and address, then gives me a tight smile. "See you later."

I'm on my way out the door when Hilary from the office staff catches me.

"Hey, Elsy," she calls, and I backtrack a few steps. "I forgot to tell you about the gala."

"Oh?"

Most symphonies will host two or three galas a year. They're formal affairs with an elaborate dinner, silent auctions, dancing, and speeches. There are limited performances with small ensembles throughout the evening rather than the full orchestra, so we get to mingle with patrons and politely ask them to empty their wallets, all while wearing fancy gowns and tuxedos.

"Should I mark you down for a plus-one?" Hilary asks.

My stomach twists. I used to go to these types of things alone, so Stephen and I could sneak off to a quiet alcove whenever we could make the time for a few frantic moments. All those storage-closet hookups made our forbidden romance all the more exciting, but when we actually had a moment alone together with our clothes on, all the excitement fizzled away.

I won't be making that mistake twice.

Opening my mouth to turn her down, I'm surprised when instead, I tell her, "Sure."

She doesn't blink, merely makes a note on her tablet. "Great. I'll get everything set up for you. Welcome to Austin."

four

. . .

Wyatt

TRAINING CAMP IS a grueling ordeal after resting all summer. Although my break was considerably shorter than some of my new teammates'. Austin splashed out of the second round of the playoffs.

Coach Curtis "Mack" MacKenzie is in his mid-fifties, stocky and bald, with a genuine smile on his face. Even when he's haranguing the team, he does it with a smile. It takes skill.

We're still getting our legs moving after some time off, so it's not unexpected that as a group we're more uncoordinated than a two-year-old on the ice for the first time. The Aces were aggressive at the start of the free agency period, trading for a few big names and signing a half dozen more.

Viggy held a handful of Captain's Practices over the last few weeks, so I've skated with some of the guys, but I wouldn't say I know any of them particularly well. And nowhere near as well as Viggy seemed to know Elsy last week. The idea curls my lip into a sneer and automatically makes me dislike the guy, which is unfair since he's genuinely been welcoming to me and the other new guys.

Henry, the center on my line, gives me a nod as we skate laps. "You settling in, Whit?"

"Getting there."

He gives me a toothy grin. "Heard you brought a girl to the bar."

Rolling my eyes, I ignore the taunt in his voice. "Just a friend."

"So you don't mind if I make a play?" He waggles his eyebrows, sounding every bit as sleazy as his reputations leads me to believe.

A low growl rumbles in my chest at the idea of playboy Luke Henry putting his dirty paws on Elsy. I don't like that, not one bit.

"Off. Limits," I grind out, glaring.

"Okay, okay," he says, raising his hands in the air. "Just trying to get the lay of the land. Maybe get laid."

"Well, find someone else to screw."

Henry laughs. "Someone's a little uptight. I think maybe you're the one who needs to get laid."

Fuck. How long has it been?

It's been years since my last actual relationship. During the season, it's usually easier to get by with a friends-with-benefits situation. I don't have the time, or, frankly, the mental energy, to deal with the emotional drain of a relationship. Throughout the playoff run, I kept it in my pants for the sake of superstition, and the last time before that was…

Damn. I don't even remember.

Last January, I was in Boston for a road game. Bex and I went out to her favorite bar and she tried to set me up with one of her friends. But I wasn't feeling it.

Mostly because Elsy was there.

She was wearing tight jeans, a navy-blue blouse, and fuck-me heels that made me want to run my hands all over her body and never let her go. Her hair was tied back in a complicated braid and she kept fidgeting with the end. Her bright, cherry-red lipstick did dangerous things to my heart rate.

So, no, I wasn't interested in hooking up with whatever her name was. I don't even remember what she looked like.

It's not like I have *feelings* for Elsy. Gross. She just gets under my skin. It bothers me she's held a grudge against me all these years. And it's not like I can blame her. What I said was fucking awful. Why won't she let me make it up to her, though? Why can't she see that I'm not the same loud-mouth, insecure kid I was back then?

A whistle blows, echoing around the rink, before Coach changes the practice lines. On the left wing is Riley, or as Viggy's named him, *Puppy*. He looks like one, with uncoordinated limbs and an overeager attitude that should be off-putting. Except we've all been rookies before, and the ones who make it are the ones who put in the effort. When new guys come in and think the team owes them a roster spot, they typically flame out.

Unless they're legacies. In which case… sometimes, they get a roster spot and *then* flame out. Publicly.

Henry is a legacy, but I don't hold it against him. He can't help who his family is and puts in the work to prove he's not skating by on his last name and pedigree. He's part of the Henry dynasty—his grandfather had a storybook career, his dad and two uncles played, and two of his brothers are in the league now. Sebastian is a goalie for Boston, and Joseph is a forward in Seattle. The youngest brother, Michael, was drafted to Vancouver at the start of summer and is killing it in the NCAA.

Joe was a year ahead of me in the national development program. We spent the last two years of high school living with billet families, going to school in the morning and training all afternoon. It was a lot of work. I almost flamed out myself. With the help of the coaching staff, I turned my grades around and passed my classes with good enough grades that I could stay on the team.

I got a college hockey scholarship by the skin of my teeth, dropping out after the second year when Philly called me up to play in the big leagues. I don't miss school, and I won't be going back to finish my degree. My sister, the PhD, has enough for the both of us.

After practice, we cool down and hit the showers. The locker room is loud and chaotic, but I mostly keep to myself since I'm still finding my place here. I know it will come with time, but the uncertainty is setting off my anxiety. Starting over keeps me off-kilter enough that I can't settle in the way I want to. It's like I'm skating with dull blades on well-scratched ice, unable to keep my balance no matter how much I try.

"Want to grab a drink?" Henry asks as we get dressed in athletic shorts and performance team T-shirts. After a decade of wearing scarlet and silver, it's difficult to get used to my entire casual wardrobe being navy and gold.

I hesitate to answer. I'm used to being left alone. In Philly, the guys knew I wasn't big on socializing, and they didn't get upset when I'd bow out of their get-togethers. Of which there were many.

But this team is new to me. I need to get along with the guys, and especially with the players on my line.

"How about dinner instead?" I offer. "I'm trying to cut back on the booze."

"Good call," Henry says. "You find some places you like yet?"

I shake my head. I've only been in town about three weeks. It's not enough to really explore the city.

"Got it. I'll give you the full tour, then," he declares. "Pick you up at seven. Text me your address."

With a sigh, I send it to him. I don't want to go out, and I definitely don't want to be chauffeured around town. He's probably smart, offering to drive; if it were up to me, I'd probably get cold feet and cancel at the last minute. Sometimes being around people is too draining to deal with.

But when I get to my condo in a swanky high-rise, the last thing I want to do is be at home by myself. I consider firing up my video game console, but even my favorite pastime doesn't interest me.

My second favorite is a bust too. Hard to have sex when, again, I don't know anybody in town. Although…

What's Elsy up to? She doesn't have anyone in this city, either.

Immediately, I dismiss the thought. She won't want to hang out with me. Especially not to have sex. And I *definitely* don't want her around Henry.

five

. . .

Elsy

THE BISTRO PUB IS A CASUAL, trendy place close to the symphony hall. On a street lined with more upscale restaurants, this one seems more low-key. The lighting is low, but still bright enough I can see the menu, and the music is enough to drown out the noise of the other diners without being so obnoxious we can't talk.

Anastasia stands as I approach, giving me a smile. "You made it."

"Thank you for inviting me."

"Being new in town is hard." Her smile turns sympathetic. "If I didn't have my partner, I don't think I'd have survived the transition."

"Oh? Where did you move from?"

"Dallas by way of Scottsdale," she says. "I've been here for six, no, seven years now. Been with the symphony for five." Anastasia laughs and shakes her head, her chestnut hair bouncing. "I'm finally getting a feel for the place."

The waiter comes by, and since she orders a glass of wine, I order myself a cocktail, too. I rarely drink two days in a row —especially after drinking a bottle of wine alone on my couch last night—but I could use the social icebreaker right now. We don't actually know each other.

She leans forward, like she's going to tell me a secret. "How do you feel about barbecue?"

My stomach twists. "It's… fine."

She laughs, clearly amused by my lack of enthusiasm. "Uh-huh."

With a sigh, I explain, "My cousins are all from Kansas City, so I grew up eating Kansas City barbecue, and it's just not my favorite. But I know Texas barbecue is supposed to be different, so I'm trying to keep an open mind."

"It's on every street corner," Anastasia says. "You won't be able to get away from it."

Looking over the menu, I'm not surprised to see barbecue on the list, but the dishes all seem to be modernized, hipster versions of the classics, knife and fork entrées with that signature Texas flare.

A shadow falls over us, and I expect it to be the waiter, lingering awkwardly.

Instead, it's Wyatt, grinning at me like he's a leopard with prey in his sights.

I think I'm supposed to be the prey in this scenario, but if there's one thing I've learned, it's that he can't prey upon me. I won't make that mistake twice.

"Eleanor," he sings, a bright smile stretching across his face.

"What are you doing here?" I grind out.

"Henry and I are here for dinner." It's only then that I notice the other tall, wide, devastatingly handsome man behind him. "He's taking me on a tour of the city."

"Great. Then continue your tour somewhere else."

The waiter hovers. "Is there a problem here?"

Wyatt grins toothily at him. "Do you mind if we combine the tables? You don't mind, do you," he says to Anastasia, who looks confused and possibly a bit concerned.

"I mind," I tell him.

"Great, perfect," Wyatt continues, ignoring me. He and Henry maneuver their table until it's joined next to ours. He slides the chair over and slips in beside me, Henry across from him.

His buddy reaches over the table to offer his hand. "Luke Henry. I've heard a lot about you."

Ah, one of the infamous Henry brothers, then.

"Elsy. I've heard of you." I keep my expression neutral. Mitch is *not* a fan of his. Something about a woman they both dated who cheated on them with a third guy.

Unwanted butterflies flutter low in my stomach as he aims his bright hockey smile my way, missing tooth and all. "Only good things, I hope."

"Not exactly."

Henry shrugs. "You win some, you lose some." He turns to the woman beside him. "I'm Luke."

She eyes his hand like someone might a snake. "Anastasia."

"How do you guys know each other?" Wyatt asks, putting his arm on the back of my chair. I shove it off.

His citrus-and-cloves cologne is intense. I should be used to it by now, but when he sets his arm on my chair again and I'm treated to another wave of his intoxicating scent, it's more difficult to push him away again. Why does he have to smell so damn good? It should be illegal.

"We're in the symphony together," she clips out.

Henry looks between us curiously. "Is this, like, a date? Did we interrupt your first date?"

"I'm married." The ice in her tone could freeze Texas.

"Cool," Henry says.

Anastasia raises her eyebrows. "Cool?"

"Yeah. Monogamy is neat. Not for me," he adds. "But the concept in general is sweet. My brother loves being monogamous with his girl. I don't have to want it for myself to recognize why other people might."

Wyatt shifts in his seat. "How was your day?" he asks me.

I glare at him. "You don't care."

His eyes lose some of their brightness. "You're right. I'm just making conversation."

"My day went fine." I reached out to a few music schools about signing on as teaching staff. So far, they've all said no, but I'm sure I'll find something. "I put up some flyers in coffee shops about music lessons."

"I can see if any of the guys have kids who want to learn," Wyatt offers.

"No offense, but I don't see a three-year-old interested in learning to play the violin." Experts advise starting after the age of five, and usually after piano lessons to learn to read music. I can teach piano, but it's not my specialty.

Wyatt frowns as he breaks off a hunk of bread, setting a piece on my plate before pushing the basket toward Anastasia. "I think some of them have older kids."

"Thanks, but no thanks." I shake my head, tossing my hair over my shoulder. It smacks Wyatt on the shoulder, and he flinches. "Besides, I'd rather not have any involvement with your team."

Henry lifts his eyebrows. "Why not? The team is awesome."

Most people are champing at the bit to get closer to the professional athletes in my social circle. And yeah, some of them have egos bigger than the solar system. But when you spend time with them, you realize they're actually normal human beings who don't want to be celebrities. Nine guys out of ten only want to play hockey, regardless of the money or fame that comes with it.

Anastasia looks between them. "What team?"

"We're on the Austin Aces," Henry explains. "Whitney and I are hockey players."

"Oh." Her mouth turns down in distaste. "Sports."

The hurt look on Henry's face makes me laugh. "Not everyone is obsessed with you hockey players," I tease him. "Some of us have lives outside of watching other people chase a puck."

"Oh, like your patrons?" Wyatt cuts in. "You're performing, same as we are. The only difference is you wear a gown and your violin when we have skates and sticks."

I frown. I can't read his tone. Is he teasing, friendly, or is he taunting, mean-spirited? I hate that I can't tell with him.

The waiter interrupts, at long last bringing our drinks, while Henry and Wyatt order their own, along with our food. I suppose there's no getting out of eating dinner with them.

Wyatt reaches across me for Anastasia's menu, his arm brushing featherlight across my breast. He goes still, his face red.

Fireworks light up my body at the innocent contact. Inside my bra cup, my nipple pebbles, and heat flares through me to coil deep in my belly. At least I'm wearing a cardigan over my blouse. Hopefully, nobody will see it.

"Sorry," he mutters.

I try to pretend like I'm unaffected. "What's a boob graze between enemies?"

His face falls. "Is that what we are?"

"Well, it's not like we're friends," I point out.

Wyatt doesn't look happy about that, either. A muscle clenches in his jaw. "So you default to enemies?"

How do I tell him I have every reason to despise him? I honestly can't decide which part makes me hate him more: that he was an insensitive asshat while publicly discussing our sex life, or that I was so meaningless to him he couldn't remember who I was.

It's not like the sex was life changing. It was good. He was attentive and took care to ensure I had a good time. Multiple times, if I remember correctly.

But the cruelty of his comments the next morning wiped away anything good about our night together. And that, I can't forget.

Maybe one day, I'll be able to forgive, but I won't forget.

six

. . .

Wyatt

I FUCKED UP.

I don't know what I did, but I know I fucked up.

Elsy and I lead very different lives, but considering I'm the only person she knows in the city, I thought she'd be reaching out to do something.

But I should have known my butterfly would spread her wings and fly. It's difficult to keep her down for very long.

I try to text her half a dozen times, but everything I type seems stupid. I don't want to come on too strong, but I don't want to scare her off, either.

Another invitation to a team event would probably be a good way to hang out. She could meet the other wives and partners. There's a reality TV show filming the team right now and there are always a bunch of staffers hanging around.

I don't know why I'm so invested in spending time with Elsy. It's more than Bex asking me to look out for her. I *want* to. I want to protect her, to make sure she's okay.

When she said we were enemies the other night, it was like something in me broke. As much as I enjoy needling her, I thought we were having fun. It was all a game. I didn't think she actually *hated* me...

Throughout training camp, she's on my mind, and I'm not playing well. It's a good thing I've been doing this for nine years and can operate on muscle memory, because no matter how much I try to compartmentalize and focus on hockey, she keeps creeping in.

Viggy pulls me aside in the locker room. "Want to talk about it?" he asks. He's not my friend, he's my captain, and I know it's not a conversation I can opt out of.

Still, I'll try.

"Talk about what?"

He sighs. "Whatever has you so twisted up, you're playing like a rookie again."

Frustration twists my stomach, centered in a heavy knot behind my ribs, and I drag my hand down my face. "Is it that obvious?"

"Yeah, man." His laugh is short and forced. "Is it the reality show thing? Do I need to go to Coach?"

Shaking my head, I push my hair off my forehead. "Nah. They're not bothering me." The cameras aren't allowed in here when we're changing, and I don't have any juicy gossip to interest them. Mostly, they leave me alone. I'm nothing but another nameless, faceless blob to them—which is exactly how I want it.

Being the focus of a reality TV show? Kill me now. Make it swift.

"So what is it?" Viggy asks.

"It's nothing."

Understanding dawns, and his expression clears. "So it's a chick."

My face twists into a scowl. "She's not a chick." She's a fully grown woman who deserves to be treated with respect.

"It's serious, then."

I swallow my hesitation and confide in my captain. "She called us enemies."

"And you don't hate her?"

"She's—I—" I sigh. "No, I don't hate her." Not in the slightest.

I'm not saying I'm in love with her. I wouldn't go that far. She's a cool person with an even cooler vibe. I've been able to catch glimpses of her—the real her—from a distance over the years. When she lets her guard down, she's…

"She has this way of drawing everyone in," I tell him. "Elsy cares about people, like, genuinely cares about them and not just for show. She goes out of her way to help her friends. She'll drop everything for them." I sigh. "But I'm not one of her friends."

"That's tough, man." His hand lands heavy on my shoulder, the sympathy I didn't know I was looking for.

"Any advice?" Holding my breath, I lean closer to him.

Viggy snorts. "Fuck, you think I know what to do? There's a reason I stay single. Easier that way."

Everything in me deflates. "Thanks, man. Really appreciate it."

He shrugs. "Invite her to a game. Maybe with her in the stands, you won't suck so much."

Flipping him off, I turn back to my locker to strip off my sweaty gear. As unhelpful as he was, inviting her to a game probably isn't a bad idea. She's a hockey fan, right? Her best friend plays. She probably knows other guys in the league, too, guys she's met through him. She can catch up with them.

Wait. I do *not* want her to get cozy with any of them. Maybe I shouldn't invite her after all…

Can't believe I'm even thinking this, but I wish my sister was here. She'd know what to do.

The lit-up screen taunts me as I hover my finger over Bex's contact in my phone. I don't want to reach out to her. She'd be able to see right through me and tell me to do what I already know I should.

No. I should just invite Elsy to the game. I'll get her friend tickets, too. That way, she won't be alone.

Before I can second, triple, and quadruple guess myself, I email the admin staff and request three tickets to the game. It's preseason, so we're not expecting full attendance, but I still have to arrange it in advance. Players are allotted so many tickets for each home game, as long as we coordinate with the front office. I'll leave it up to Elsy if she'd rather sit at ice level or up in the suite with the other wives and partners.

Going about my day, I see the trainers for treatment on my shoulder and film a quick confessional-style video with the TV crew. They want us to do these videos once or twice a week, or when something drama-worthy happens. I'm not sure how I feel about being part of a reality TV show. I just want to play hockey.

I'm driving home for the day when my phone buzzes with the reply from admin: three tickets acquired. I text them to Elsy without comment.

Immediately, my phone rings over the Bluetooth connection.

"What the fuck, Wyatt?" she demands.

"What's up, Elizabeth?" I aim for calm, cool, and collected, but I don't think the gravel in my voice hides how turned on I get when she says my name in that snippy, pissed-off tone. This game we're playing, when I call her everything but her name, is a surefire way to set her off.

She makes everything inside me light up. My cock perks up, too. It's like a Pavlovian response to the mettle in her voice. It's fucked how much I enjoy being tortured by her.

"Why did you send me tickets to your game?"

"Oh, so you got them." My smile stretches across my face as I hang a left and head toward her apartment instead of mine.

Elsy makes a frustrated noise. "Yeah. Why'd you send me three tickets?"

"Thought you and Anastasia might want to come to a game. She's married, so tell her to bring her spouse."

It didn't escape my notice that Anastasia was very careful with pronouns at dinner. I don't know if her partner is male, female, or nonbinary, nor do I care. Hockey is for everyone; I genuinely believe that. I don't care about the color of anyone's skin or who they love. It shouldn't matter. That it does in this day and age drives me absolutely nuts. It's terrible that some people don't feel safe enough to be who they are and live their lives out loud.

"I don't want to go to your game," Elsy snaps.

Flinching, I thank my lucky puck that she's on a voice call and not video. I don't need her to remind me exactly how much she dislikes me.

"You don't have to come," I say evenly. "I thought it might be something fun to do with your friend."

"Why are you like this?"

"Like what?"

"So… so…" She grunts. "Just stop it, okay?"

I smile. "Stop what, exactly?"

"You know what you're doing." She sounds so frustrated. I wonder what it would take for her to snap.

"I don't, though."

Pulling into the parking lot of the little deli around the corner from her apartment, I place a takeout order on my phone.

"You home?" I ask when she doesn't say anything.

"Why?" She's so suspicious.

"Just making conversation." While they prepare my order, I tilt my seat back and relax. "How was rehearsal?"

"Fuck off, Wyatt," she snaps.

"Ouch, Eleanor. I'm really feeling the love."

"You don't care, so don't pretend like you do. I don't know what your end game is here, but I'm not going to fall at your feet just because you act like a decent human being for once in your goddamn life."

My chest pangs.

"Is that what you think I want?" I can hear the pain in my voice. Can she? I hope not. "Do you really think this is only a game to me?"

"Isn't it?"

The call disconnects.

Fuck. I messed that up. Hell, I'm messing *everything* up.

Darting inside the deli, I pick up the order and drive the short distance to her apartment.

Her building is gated, a squat five floors centered around a resort-style pool with cabanas and loungers. There are pickleball, tennis, and basketball courts. It's the kind of bougie place my sister would love, but I didn't think Elsy would go after all these upscale amenities.

Someone is leaving as I walk in, so I nod and they hold the door open.

Making my way up to the fourth floor, I shake out my shoulders and take a breath to steady myself. It'll be okay. Although I have no idea why I'm here. This is probably a terrible idea, but it'll all work out.

I just need to get my head in the game.

seven

. . .

Elsy

THE KNOCK on my door startles me, making me knock over my nail polish onto the vinyl flooring.

"Just a minute," I call, as I frantically reach for the tissues on my coffee table. I do my best to mop up the blood-red polish before it can stain, then hobble with wet toes to the front door.

I'm expecting a delivery, or maybe my cute neighbor with more of my mail that keeps getting delivered to his box.

Instead, I find the hulking form of Wyatt, devil incarnate. He's wearing an Aces T-shirt and is probably fresh from the arena. He smells good, too. Fuck. Why does he always have to smell so damn good?

"What are you doing here?" I demand.

"Brought you dinner." He holds up a bag from the deli— the same one he brought food from the day he helped me move in.

My eyes narrow with suspicion. "Why?"

Especially after I hung up on him. His showing up here is the last thing I expected.

His bulky shoulders jump with a shrug. "You need to eat."

Is that a dig at my size? I know I'm fat; I don't need him to point it out.

"Come on," he says, more softly now. "Let me in, Elspeth."

I grunt. "Don't call me that."

Against my better judgment, I step aside and let him into my apartment. He looks around with interest. I'm almost fully unpacked and have started decorating. There are stools for my kitchen counter now, along with throw pillows and blankets on the couch.

Wyatt beelines to the counter, unloading the bag of take-out. He rummages through my cabinets, too, pulling out plates and finding forks in the drawer. I'm surprised by the care he takes as he plates our food.

"What are you doing here?" I ask again.

Instead of answering, he slides a plate across the counter for me as I sit.

"I got you tuna salad on a croissant," he says. "I thought maybe you didn't like their sourdough."

"Croissants are… good." Why is it I'm always so tongue-tied around him? I can hardly think straight.

He has two turkey sandwiches for himself. One has a salad, the other has a plate of fries. He puts two-thirds of the fries on my plate, plus the pickle from each of his entrées. Mine already has a small container of potato salad.

I stare at him. "What are you doing?"

Wyatt cocks his head. "Do you not want fries?"

"They're yours."

"I can't eat all of them. Not on my nutrition plan."

My forehead pinches into a frown. I'm missing something. None of this makes sense.

"I want you to have them," he continues. "Just because I have to be strict about what I eat doesn't mean you have to, too."

"Why would it?" It's not like we make a habit out of eating together.

His broad shoulders lift as he shrugs, the movement serving to remind me how massive he is. "I thought you'd like them. That's why I ordered them," he says. "If you don't want them, don't eat them."

It's not about the fries.

Or maybe it is.

I don't know.

"Do you have a tuxedo?" I blurt out.

Slowly, Wyatt swivels his head to look at me. "Yes?"

"What are you doing on Saturday?"

A Cheshire smile spreads over his face. "Elsy, are you asking me on a date?"

"No!"

He waits, his eyes bright. Is he mocking me?

I blow out a breath. "The symphony gala is Saturday and I have a plus-one."

Wyatt waits patiently. When I don't continue, he says, "And you want me to go with you?"

"I mean, you have a tux already." It makes sense, in some weird, twisted, roundabout way.

Besides, he's the only person I know in this city. And I'm not about to ask Luke Henry to go with me. No.

The air is thick with tension as I meet his eyes. It kills me to have to ask anyone for help. Of all the people in the world, the fact it's him particularly rankles. Slowly, he nods. "I do have a tux."

"And you don't have a game," I add.

"We play Friday night and Sunday matinee. So I wouldn't be able to party too hard on Saturday night," he drawls.

"Yes, because a symphony gala is probably on par with partying it up in a club until three o'clock in the morning."

Wyatt grins. "I haven't done that since my second year in the league."

I roll my eyes. "So, will you do it?"

"Sure, Elsy," he says, his voice warm and rumbly, making my heart rate ricochet sky high. "I'll be your date to the gala."

————

I shouldn't be here. But because Wyatt agreed to accompany me to the gala, I couldn't make myself say no to attending his game. I'm supporting my new local team. That's all it is.

I don't *hate* hockey. I like it better when Mitch is playing, sure, but the sport itself isn't boring. It can even be fun. My issue is with the hockey *players*. I liked going to games a lot more before Wyatt crashed into my life and set my self-esteem into a downward spiral. Even though it's been years, I'm still not fully recovered.

I don't have any Aces gear, and I'm *definitely* not wearing Wyatt's name on my back, so I pull on a Boston Grizzlies sweatshirt that Vanessa, my old roommate, gave me. Several of my friends are dating players or staff members with the team, so it's safe to say I spent a lot of time with the Grizzlies.

… and now I'm about to spend time with the Aces. It's clear Wyatt won't leave me alone, so I might as well get used to the idea now.

Anastasia wasn't able to join me for the game since she already had plans, so I sent Wyatt the two unused tickets. I don't know what to do with them. It's not like I have anyone else to invite to the game. And I'm not about to walk up to perfect strangers and invite them to hang out.

Mitch calls me as I'm walking into the arena.

"It's like you know when I'm about to do something wrong," I tell him as I scan my ticket.

His hearty laugh echoes through my phone. "What are you doing?"

"I'm at an Aces game."

My best friend growls. "Fuck off. No, you're not."

"I am."

"Please tell me you're at least wearing my sweater," he says. "I can't wait to see the look on that fuckhead's face when you wear my name."

"I'm not," I laugh.

Mitch falls quiet. "You're not wearing his?"

"Nah. The Grizzlies jacket."

"Oh. Okay. That's okay, then," he decides. He has some buddies on the team. And considering the way my friends started dating their players, there's a lot of overlap between his friends and mine. The Grizzlies guys always treated me like part of the club, another little sister to look after.

It was… nice. I felt protected. Appreciated.

With Wyatt, though… I don't feel the same. It's infantilizing with him. He's not treating me like an equal, but as someone inferior.

And I am *not* inferior to him in any way, shape, or form. I know my worth, even if he doesn't recognize it.

As I make my way to the stands, Mitch and I catch up. He has a game tonight in Nashville, then flies back to New Orleans for a home match against Tampa the next day. He's coming and going so much, I can barely keep track. If it weren't for the automated calendar alerts for his team on my phone, I would never know where he was.

We've been friends since our first semester of college. Our dorms were next to each other and our roommates were fucking, so when she would go to his, he would come to mine and we'd hang out for a few hours. It was a mutually beneficial arrangement. He took me under his wing. The music department threw great parties, and the hockey team never stopped partying, so it was a match made in heaven.

I was there for him when his mom died, and he was there for me when my parents split up. We're friends, good friends, but we've never been more. The idea of something romantic with Mitch is almost gross. He's the closest thing I've ever had to a brother.

My ex-boyfriends haven't always understood that. His ex-girlfriends—few as they were—couldn't get comfortable with knowing our friendship comes first. We don't sleep in the same bed when either of us are dating someone, but if we're both single? Fair game. He's perpetually touch-starved and I'm a big fan of physical affection. It's my love language. It's like we were made for each other. Platonically.

Which is probably why he's never forgiven Wyatt for what he did. As glad as I am that he's on my side, sometimes I wonder if the reason I haven't been able to move past it is because Mitch hasn't, either.

My seats are at ice level, right behind the Aces' bench. Today's game is against the Colorado Dragons. My friend Viv's brother Chuck is on the team, and as he skates past for warm-ups, he gives me a nod. We've met a few times, but we aren't close. Enough to pick each other out of a crowd. I'll say hello to him after the game, but we don't need to go for a drink or anything. We're not that kind of friends. Acquaintances, really.

My eyes linger on number 17. Wyatt looks good in the navy and gold. He stands tall on his skates, carrying himself with confidence. When he catches sight of me, he stumbles to a stop, and my heart skips a beat.

Why the hell does he have to be so fucking attractive?

And worse, why do I have to be attracted to *him*? Of all the guys in the world, why does it have to be him who gets my engine going?

A slow smile spreads over his face before he sends me a wink. My entire body heats from within until I think I'm about to combust.

Another player shoves him forward, and Wyatt shakes his head, returning to his laps. He looks over his shoulder at me as he skates, stick handling a puck like the professional he is before driving it toward the net.

The goalie, Rempel, doesn't try to block it. The missile lands in the back of the net with textbook precision, and my panties get a little wet.

Fuck. This will be a *long* game.

eight

. . .

Wyatt

ELECTRICITY CRACKLES through every inch of my body after the game. I landed a goal and two assists; I was on fucking *fire*. After a lackluster training camp, I finally feel like I'm settling in—with the team, with my line, with my *life*.

It's because Elsy was in the stands. I'm sure of it. Now I'll have to figure out how to get her here for every game.

After speeding through my cool-down, I hurry the reporters through the post-game media circus. Agitation and adrenaline war in my bloodstream as I finally take my shower. I dress in my game-day suit and head for the long hallway, where we can meet up with friends and family. I told Elsy to meet me here and left her name with the admin. Still, a part of me is worried that she won't. And then I'm confused because why should I care if she doesn't show up?

Walking into the hall with Henry on my heels, I find Elsy talking to Chuck Gallagher. She's wearing a Grizzlies sweatshirt with—are those signatures? Did the entire fucking Grizzlies team sign her jacket? Oh, no, that won't do at all.

"Eleanor," I greet, giving her a nod, then turn a wary eye to my opponent. "Gallagher."

"Whitney." He nods back. "Good game."

"Yeah, you too."

When he offers his hand, I shake it.

"I was just inviting Elsy for a drink," he says, almost self-consciously. "You want to join us?" He looks behind me to where Henry's lingering, obviously eavesdropping, without forcing his way into the conversation. "Is this some kind of situation you three are keeping under wraps?"

Elsy makes a face. "Ew. Gross. No."

My stomach twists at her blatant dismissal. I would never want to share her with anyone, much less Henry. Besides, we're not together. She can hardly stand to look at me. "Yeah, no. But if you want to grab a drink, the team's getting together at the pub."

Henry steps in. "I'd love for you to join us, Elsy." His voice is as smooth as crushed velvet—and not in a good way. It's almost sleazy, coming from him. I haven't seen him like that before.

She shudders. "Yeah, I'm going to need you to stop talking now," she tells him, and he frowns.

"You need a ride?" I ask her.

"I'm going to take an Uber," she says with a pinched look on her face. "Chuck, you want to ride with me?"

"I'll drive you," I say before he can open his mouth.

He gives me a flat look.

"Both of you," I mumble. "C'mon. My car's this way."

Henry doesn't bother to hide his laugh. "See you there."

The parking garage is attached to the arena, and the valet attendants have brought around all the players' cars for us. I open the door and Elsy slips past me into the front seat with a murmured *thanks*.

Gallagher lingers outside the car. "What's the deal here?"

"What do you mean?"

"I'm not trying to make a play on her," he deadpans. "She's friends with my sister."

"Well, she's friends with *my* sister, too." *So there.*

He crosses his arms over his chest, unimpressed. "So you're pissing all over her?"

"I don't kink shame, but I'm not into water sports, dude."

Gallagher rolls his eyes. "Seriously, Whitney. I'm not into her."

Automatically, my hackles go up. "Why not? She's fucking hot."

I'd have to be blind not to see that.

"Just not my type." He shrugs. "All I want to do is check in on her so Viv doesn't rip my head off. That's all this is."

Our conversation cut off by Elsy rolling down the window.

"Are you two going to gossip all day, or can we get going?"

"Yes, Your Highness," I tease, and she scowls as she rolls the window back up.

"Oh. So it's like that," Gallagher says with a knowing grin.

"Like what?"

"You have a thing for her."

My mouth drops open. "What?"

He laughs. "Yeah. You're totally into her." He ducks into the back seat.

As I round the car, I wonder if that's true. No. It can't be. Just because we hooked up all those years ago doesn't mean I want to do it again.

Except… I kind of do. She's hot as fuck. She's bigger than she was thirteen years ago, but I happen to like her curves. I like a woman with some meat on her bones.

But it doesn't mean I'm *into* her. She's prickly. I don't want to be stabbed in the kidney—or anywhere else, for that matter. If I have feelings…

No. I don't have feelings for her. That's ridiculous.

As I slide into the driver's seat, I'm treated to the subtle floral scent of her perfume. Jasmine, I think. Normally, perfume makes me sneeze, but something about the light wisp of her scent makes my pulse throb.

Elsy's already buckled in, so I reach over and turn the A/C up high for her. She's clutching a plastic airsick bag.

"Already nauseous?"

"Around you? Always," she mutters, looking out the window.

Gallagher stifles a snicker.

The guys are already seated when we arrive. A few of the other Dragons players have joined in, too. Henry has commandeered a small table for four next to the group, and it's there that Elsy goes, so I amble after her.

I feel awkward and uncoordinated without my skates. Off-kilter. Like I'm missing a limb.

She takes the seat across from Henry, and I slide in beside her. She's not a small woman, so our thighs touch on the sticky booth material, and it sends my stomach on a roller coaster.

I must be hungry. That's it.

Tina, the waitress usually assigned to our section, beelines over to us. She's good at keeping the fans away from us and letting us relax after a game.

"Hey, sugar," she says, cocking her hip. "What can I get you?"

"Water, please," I request. "Elizabeth, you drinking?"

"Around you? Always," she mutters again.

My blood rushes south at the annoyance on her face, my pulse throbbing. Fuck, her petulant quips get me going like nothing else.

"Tito's and Sprite, please, too," I tell Tina. "She wants a cheeseburger, no tomato or ketchup, with a side of barbecue sauce, please."

Elsy glares at me. "I'm perfectly capable of ordering for myself."

"I know." I turn back to Tina. "Same for me, but I'm good with ketchup."

"Burger sounds good," Chuck says. "I'll have the same."

Henry nods. "Yeah, same here."

Elsy elbows me directly under my rib cage. "Move over. You're taking up too much space."

In response, I move closer to her until our thighs are plastered together from hip to knee.

Her eyes narrow as she aims a lethal glare my way.

Heart racing, I grin back at her, unrepentant.

She picks up her fork, her hand curling around the utensil like it's a spear. Or maybe a shiv. I wouldn't put it past her to stab me in the junk with the tines. Hurriedly, I scoot away to give her some breathing room, and she puts the fork back down.

"So your name is Elizabeth?" Henry asks her. "Like, your real name."

She scowls at me, when he's the one who asked the question, and I lift my eyebrows at her.

"My name is Elsy," she says evenly.

"But he called you Elizabeth."

"He has problems with his memory," she snaps. "He knows I don't like it and does it anyway."

My entire body tenses. Is that what she thinks is happening?

"I thought you liked it," I whisper. "It's our little game."

"No, Wyatt," Elsy says, a hint of steel in her voice. "I've never once liked it. In fact, I seem to remember telling you not to call me those names. Multiple times."

"I thought it was—it was a game. Like the way you…"

She shakes her head. "It's not a game to me."

Swallowing, I meet her eyes. "Okay. I won't do it anymore. Elsy."

"Thank you." She crosses her arms over her chest,

drawing my eyes down again. It takes everything in me to focus on her face.

"So," Henry shouts, clearly ready to change the subject. "You're friends with Mitchell in New Orleans, and clearly you know a Dragon, and you're wearing a signed Grizzlies jacket. Who the hell are you?"

Elsy shrugs. "I'm just a girl from Ohio."

"At least you didn't go to Ohio State," I mutter.

Having attended Michigan for three and a half semesters, I still take the greatest rivalry in sports seriously. It's in my blood. My dad was a Michigan man, my sister took the lacrosse team to the national championship twice in her four years, and I loved my time playing hockey there. It's not my mom's fault she went to Nebraska on a cheer scholarship and couldn't be like the rest of us.

Gallagher shakes his head. "She's friends with my sister. I promised Viv I'd keep an eye out for her."

"And I told *you*, I'm fine," Elsy says, turning her glare on him. "Viv, Bex, and all the rest of them don't need to worry about me." She sighs. "At least you don't play Boston for another few weeks. The last thing I need is Al and Jake getting all aflutter."

My eyebrows dart up. "Who?"

"Al is my future brother-in-law," Gallagher says with a laugh. "His brother is dating my sister."

"That doesn't make him your brother-in-law," Henry says. "He's your sister's brother-in-law."

Gallagher shrugs. "He's family."

"He's an overprotective golden retriever with the brains of an orange cat," Elsy mutters. "Nice guy, but kind of dumb."

"Sounds like most hockey players, then," Henry says.

"No. Not in my experience." She glares at me again. "He's actually a good guy."

Because in her estimation, I'm not.

"My brother just got traded to Boston last summer,"

Henry says. "Maybe you know him. Sebastian Henry? He's the goaltender."

Elsy nods slowly. "He's part of the tandem with Jake, who's dating my friend Rachel. I've met Seb's girlfriend, Audrey. Isn't she related to the coach?"

"His daughter, yeah." Henry grins. "Aren't they sickening?"

"Kind of," she admits.

"So you're, like, *in* with the hockey teams," he says. "What brings you to Austin? And would you like to adopt another hockey team?"

Her small smile dies, her eyes belying her pain. "No."

I don't know all the details, only that she was asked to leave the Boston Symphony after a confrontation with her ex. Bex was cagey on the details, insisting it wasn't her place to tell me. Somehow, I don't think Elsy will spill her deepest, darkest secrets to me anytime soon.

"No?" Gallagher grins at her. "You want to move to Colorado?"

"Definitely not," Elsy says. "I came to Austin because I had to leave Boston, but now that I've unpacked, I'm not moving anywhere anytime soon. And no," she says to Henry, "I don't want anything to do with the hockey scene here. I have no ties to this team. That's the way it's going to stay."

nine

. . .

Elsy

WYATT IS WEARING A TUXEDO. This is not a drill. Tall, wide, built, gorgeous Wyatt Whitney is standing on my doorstep in a fucking tuxedo, holding a corsage with a deep-red rose at the center. His strawberry-blond hair is slicked back away from his ruddy, freshly shaved face.

His mouth hangs open, his face slack as he stares at me. "Elsy…"

My stomach falls. Fuck. I can't wear this dress. Clearly, it was a mistake. I thought being a little adventurous with the sequins would be a fun change, but I should have put on my boring, boxy black dress.

"Let me go change," I mutter, turning away from the door.

"Don't change," he blurts out. "Don't ever change."

It's my turn to stare at him. "What's gotten into you?"

He shakes his head. "Nothing. Just—let's go. Are you ready?"

I grab my shawl and my clutch in one hand, my violin in the other. My hand shakes as I go to lock the front door and gently, his touch so light on mine, Wyatt takes the key and locks up. He grabs my hand in his, pressing the key to my palm, and then slips the corsage onto my wrist.

"What's this?" I touch the flower petals of the three roses. They're soft as silk. The dark red looks good against the navy blue of my dress, with pops of white baby's breath and greenery to fill out the corsage.

"I thought you needed it," he says with a bashful little grin. "You look great."

"Thanks. You clean up pretty well yourself."

I mean, it's not a hardship to look at him on a good day. Add in the tuxedo and the heady cologne… whew, it's a pretty powerful package.

Then again—a tuxedo on any halfway good-looking man is enough to turn up the attraction level. That Wyatt is already a solid ten on a good day…

If only he didn't have to open his mouth. Then he'd be an eleven on a scale from one to ten.

When we reach his car in the guest parking lot, he opens the door and waits for me to get in before closing it gently. He tugs at his bowtie as he climbs into the driver's seat.

"You ready?" he asks, turning to look at me. For once, he doesn't look at my boobs.

"Let's get this over with," I mutter, edging away from him and closer to the car door.

Wyatt frowns. "Okay." Is that disappointment in his tone? I can't imagine why. He probably wants this night to be over with as much as I do.

He's the one doing me the favor, and I'm already dreading what he's going to ask me to do in return. Because if I know Wyatt, he will *always* make sure I repay the favor—with interest. Going to his game the other night wasn't enough. With him, nothing ever is.

Instead of valeting the car, I direct him to the employees' parking lot. Nerves swirl in my stomach, and I'm already regretting bringing him to this thing. I could have come alone. It's work. And I have to mingle with the patrons and prove that the symphony is worth donating to.

Wyatt's hand is on the small of my back as we navigate into the building. He offered to carry my violin, but he's lucky I even let him breathe near it, so he's carrying my purse with his head held high.

Hilary, the admin in charge of corralling all the musicians, directs me where to leave my violin. My ensemble isn't performing until later this evening, so I have time to schmooze the patrons.

I love patrons. I hate schmoozing.

Small talk doesn't come naturally to me. It feels disingenuous. Yes, I care about how the person I'm talking to is doing, but I don't *know* them. It's all surface level. There's no time to actually get to know them. It's all a plea for them to open their wallets on the symphony's behalf.

It's not like I can use Wyatt as a buffer. He's a sports guy. Somehow, I doubt the people who come to our performances are the same type of people who go to his games.

But when we approach the first couple, who look to be in their mid-fifties, the man smiles wide.

"You're Wyatt Whitney," he says.

"Yes, sir, I am," Wyatt says, offering his hand for a shake. "This is Elsy Alexander. She's a violinist with the symphony."

"Oh, how lovely," the wife says. She's wearing a red velvet gown and enough diamonds to fund several small countries. Her bleached-blond hair is teased high. I guess when they said everything is bigger in Texas, they meant *everything*. Even her boobs, which, from how high they sit on her chest, have been artificially enhanced.

Hey. Live your truth. There's nothing wrong with getting a breast augmentation. Sure, if I were to do so, it would be a reduction rather than an increase, but I have no way of knowing what she looked like before.

I've considered lip fillers over the years, since mine are so narrow, but I've chickened out both times I sat in the exam room. The closest I've gotten is microneedling my brows and eyelash extensions, semi-permanent modifications that I know will fade away or can be reversed if I regret them too much. I can't wear long nails because of the violin, so I'm limited to fun polish colors, even if I almost always end up with my same color: Ruby Pumps.

Wyatt squeezes my arm, and I glance up at him, confused. He lifts one blond eyebrow.

Oh. Yeah.

Schmoozing. Patrons. Wahoo.

Out of the corner of my eye, I catch a glimpse of a man in a tuxedo. He's maybe five foot eight, with dark brown hair and a short beard, and—

Adrenaline courses through me, raising my heart rate with each pounding beat and flooding my system with an unwanted chemical reaction.

Oh, no.

No. Not now.

I thought I was getting better. I thought I was over this.

"Would you excuse us for a moment," I say politely, then drag Wyatt away before they can speak.

He removes my hand from his elbow and sets his palm on my back.

"What's going on?" he mutters as I stalk across the room.

"Not here."

"Elsy—"

"I said, not here."

Yanking open the first door I see, I scan the small closet. I throw myself inside, and Wyatt follows at a more sedate pace, closing the door behind us.

"What's going on?" he asks.

My throat constricts like it's closing. I reach for the necklace I'm wearing, fiddling with the clasp, but my fingers feel thick, clumsy.

"Can you take this off?" Panic laces my voice.

"Elsy, what's going on?" Wyatt asks. His voice sounds far away.

"Take off my fucking necklace," I snap. "I can't breathe."

His big, warm body moves behind me. It takes him a few tries, but finally the dainty silver chain falls away, and I catch it in my palm.

I take in a ragged breath, trying to work air into my lungs. It's not enough. Bending over, I set one hand on my knee, the other on the wall to brace myself.

My hair is tied up in a sleek bun that took fucking forever to do, so at least it's not loose and getting in my way. The fabric of my dress is breathable, so I don't feel too confined—not any more so than usual in my shapewear, at least. I kick off my uncomfortable heels and try to breathe.

Wyatt sets a hand on my shoulder. "Elsy, you're scaring me."

"I'm scaring me, too." I sound drunk. Or maybe high.

"Are you okay?"

A dark laugh spills past my tingling lips. "I'm on the brink of a panic attack and you're asking me if I'm okay?"

"Is that what this is?"

I glance up at him. He has his hand in his pocket, concern sketched on his face. Calm, cool, collected. Nothing fazes him.

"Yeah. They happen sometimes," I mutter.

"How can I help?"

"There's nothing you can do."

He hums, reaching for me. I'm surprised when he pulls me upright, then grabs my hand and places it over his heart.

"Can you feel that?" he whispers.

I nod. The *thump, thump, thump* of his heart is steady and strong.

"Just focus on my heartbeat. Breathe in."

Inhaling, I let my lungs expand.

"And out," he murmurs, and I exhale through my nose. "That's it. You're doing so good."

Something in me lights up at his praise, cutting through the panic tingeing my every thought.

"Breathe in again."

I inhale.

"And exhale."

I release the breath.

"You're good at this," I mutter, my eyes focused on the column of buttons lining his shirt.

"I used to get panic attacks," Wyatt admits in a calm, quiet voice. His stormy blue eyes are locked on mine.

"What?" I had no idea. Bex never mentioned anything.

He nods, holding my gaze. "Before every game. Sometimes between intermissions."

"How—but you're a professional hockey player."

"Took a lot of work to get there. Spent a lot of time with a sports psychologist. She gave me some tips." He gives me a sad smile. Then it fades. "It's hard, especially when you're in the thick of it. It feels almost impossible to overcome."

"Yeah."

"But you *can* overcome this," he says firmly. "This doesn't have to define you, it doesn't have to limit you. You can find a way to work with it, instead of against it."

"I've had panic attacks before," I snap.

He squeezes my hand, still pressed against his pec. "And you'll probably have them again. We just have to work on whatever triggered it."

I look away.

"Do you know what triggered it?" There's no pity in his voice, only concern.

"I thought I saw my ex," I mutter, looking away.

His sharp inhalation is enough of an answer.

"I'm pathetic. I know."

"Elsy, you are many things," Wyatt says. "But you are definitely not pathetic."

ten

. . .

Wyatt

MY HEART BREAKS at the pain on her face.

"Do you want to talk about it? Him?"

I don't want to listen to her talk about another man. But if that's what she needs, I'll give her the moon and more.

"He dumped me. I lost my job. And I left Boston three weeks later. What else do you want to know?"

It's damn-near impossible to swallow past the lump in my throat, and it's not because of the tie around my neck. Maybe *I'm* the one who needs to work on my breathing.

"Why Austin?"

"My mentor is the musical director here."

"That's good," I choke out.

She breathes in, then out, without my prompting her. Then does it again.

"I think I'm okay," Elsy whispers.

"Okay."

She tries to pull away, but I clutch her tighter. "I said—"

I let go of her hand and instead pull her into a hug. My arms wrap around her, and my eyes flutter shut at the simple pleasure of her body pressed against mine.

"What are you doing, Wyatt?" Her voice wavers.

"You seem like you need a hug."

Or maybe it's me who needs it.

She sighs, then slowly circles her arms around my waist and presses her cheek to my chest.

Without her heels, she's about half a foot shorter than me. The top of her head is the perfect angle for me to press a kiss there.

But if I were to do that, she'd probably knee me in the balls, so I restrain myself. Although I don't know where the urge came from to begin with. Clearly, something is wrong with me.

We stay wrapped up in each other for several minutes. It doesn't feel like I'm staring down the clock, though. It's... nice.

At long last, Elsy sighs again and pulls back.

"Will you, um—will you help me with my necklace?"

"Sure." I take the thin silver chain from her palm and drape it across her neck. Standing behind her, I have the perfect view down her dress, but I don't let myself get distracted as I hook the clasp and let it fall against her skin.

She ducks down and slips her heels back on, then straightens and squares her shoulders.

"We've got this," I tell her. "You've got this."

Offering me a faint smile, she sets her hand on my arm. "Thanks, Wyatt."

I offer my fist for a bump, same as I would any of my teammates. She stares at me for a moment before she curls her hand into a fist, bumping knuckles with me.

A thrill runs through me at the innocent contact, my heart so full it could burst. Even though she invited me tonight, it's clear she doesn't actually want to spend time with me. But when she needed help, she turned to *me*. She let her guard down and let me see her in a vulnerable position. That doesn't happen when you hate someone. Maybe I'm making headway after all.

Sticking my head into the hall, I check the coast is clear before I open the door fully and allow her to step out. Elsy brushes off her dress as she exits, her head held high.

In the light of the hallway, I catch sight of her face and pause.

"Hang on," I tell her, catching her arm.

She arches an eyebrow at me. "Excuse me?"

Tracing my thumb under her eye, I rub gently on the sensitive skin.

"What are you doing?"

I think she's holding her breath, her eyes locked on mine. Her teeth dig into her berry-red lips. I wonder what it would be like to taste them after all this time. Would it be every bit as good as my memories?

"You had a smudge." I hope I sound casual despite how my heart is beating a little faster now. "There. I got it."

"Thanks," she whispers.

Elsy stalks away, her sequined dress sparkling in the hall-way's low light, and I pick up the pace to stay by her side as we reach the atrium. Under the glow of the elaborate chande-lier, she glitters brighter than diamonds. She plucks two glasses of champagne off a nearby server's tray and hands one to me, downing her own.

"Feeling better?"

"Yes, actually." Her smile is sarcastic, no hint of her earlier mania.

When I make no move to drink the glass in my hand, she takes it back and sips it.

"You don't drink champagne?"

"I have a game tomorrow." I have to stay sober. If I drink, I won't be at my best, and I won't be able to take care of her.

"Oh, yeah. That's right."

"You going to come watch?" I glance at her out of the corner of my eye.

"Pass."

"Really? I'm here with you tonight, and you can't come to my game tomorrow?"

She makes a face. "If I really have to."

Turning to face her, I set my hand on her arm. She gives me a withering stare until I remove it. My cock twitches. Why do I love when she's mean to me? More for my therapist to unravel.

"Do you really not want to go? You don't have to. I was—"

Elsy looks down, then meets my eyes. Nerves dance over her face. "I don't know anyone."

"I can introduce you to the other wives and partners," I offer. A few of my teammates are queer, though they're not in public relationships at the moment. Still, I make a point to keep my language inclusive. It's not my business if someone isn't ready to come out. The last thing I'd want is to make someone feel unwanted.

I've got enough experience with that, thanks.

She shakes her head. "But I'm not a wife or a partner. I'm nobody. I have no relation to the team."

"You have me. Isn't that enough?"

Her gaze narrows as she focuses on something behind me. "Is that—what are they doing here?"

"Who?"

She nods behind me. "Did you put them up to this?"

Looking over my shoulder, I find a cluster of hockey players near the hors d'oeuvres table.

"I didn't tell them about this." It's the honest truth.

"So they showed up of their own accord?"

"I… guess so."

When Henry invited me over to grab dinner and play video games, I told him I was coming to this thing. And Viggy knew because I asked him where the nearest dry cleaner was.

But Puppy and the rest of the guys… I have no idea.

"I didn't invite them," I tell her quietly.

Elsy's baby blues search mine. Finally, she nods. "I believe you."

"Maybe they're fans of the arts? They're patrons?"

Her tinkling laugh is like music to my ears. It's clear she doesn't think so. Neither do I, truth be told.

"I'll get them to clear out," I promise. Though I don't know how…

"It's fine. They're here. They can be a buffer," she says. "Hell, maybe they'll be able to convince more people to donate."

"Here's hoping," I mutter, before the crowd descends upon us.

"Elsy," Henry says, stepping forward and brushing a kiss against her cheek. "You look lovely."

"Thanks," she says, her cheeks pink. "You are… adequate."

He gives her a lopsided grin. "You're falling in love with me. Admit it."

"Yeah, I don't think that's what's happening," Viggy says, cuffing him on the back of the head.

"Didn't bring your TV crew?" I tease him.

The captain's withering glare would strike fear in a lesser man, but competing on the same side of the ice every day has dulled some of its potency. "I could barely get away from them."

"What's this about a TV crew?" Elsy asks.

"They're filming a reality TV show about the team," I explain. "The producer is kind of obsessed with Viggy. It's adorable."

"She's the worst," he insists.

Elsy giggles. Some of the color is returning to her cheeks. "I'm sure she's not that bad."

Viggy scowls.

"What're you guys doing here?" I change the subject.

"Your girl's performing tonight," Henry says, throwing his arm around my shoulders. I shove him off, and he smirks at me. "She's part of the team, too, whether she admits it or not. We came to support her."

"She's not my girl," I mutter. Though I can't deny the warmth that spreads through me at the thought.

Wait. That's weird. Elsy has never been and will never be mine. I made sure of that when I fucked up all those years ago.

Besides, I don't *want* her to be mine. Right? Just because I enjoy antagonizing her doesn't mean I want anything else.

If she wanted to sleep with me, sure, I'd go there again. I'd show her all the ways I've changed. But—

Fuck.

"I need a drink." Stalking off, I go in search of the bar. There has to be more than champagne here.

Puppy falls into step beside me. "She's pretty," he says.

My booming laugh echoes throughout the atrium, drawing attention from curious patrons. "She's out of your league, man."

"I can look. Doesn't mean I'm going to touch." He gives a short laugh. "Besides, Henry and Cap have already laid down the law. Last thing I want to do is mess with team dynamics by going after your girl."

"She's not my girl," I say again.

"You just want her to be," he finishes.

I glare at him. "Shut up."

He shakes his head, amusement written on his face. "You're so fucking obvious, bud."

We reach the bar and I order a scotch and soda to take the edge off. So much for that whole *not drinking the night before a game* promise I made. I want to get Elsy a drink, too, but since she's performing tonight, plus she's on the heels of her panic attack, so I don't think that's a good idea. Not after she slammed two glasses of champagne. I order her a Coke instead.

"Don't even think about it," I warn Puppy when he opens his mouth. He's only nineteen. "Coach will kill you if you get busted drinking. The newspaper's society reporter is here tonight. I'm sure it won't take long for them to figure out who you are."

"I know, I know." He orders a Coke, too.

Together, we wait for our drinks.

"You doing okay?"

He nods. "Ready for the season to start for real." We have three more preseason games. He's still borderline and could be sent down to the minors any day now.

"Shitting bricks?" Personally, I think he'll stay in the big club, but I still remember those early days, always wondering when the other shoe would drop.

"Something like that." He gives a sarcastic smile. "I just want to know where I'm going to be. Will they keep me up with the team or send me down to the farm team? I want to stay up, I want to prove that I can do this."

"Then you will." I cuff him on the shoulder. "Just do your best. That's all we're asking."

Puppy hums. "Yeah. Thanks, man."

"What are teammates for?"

Our drinks are ready and I slip a twenty into the tip jar before we weave through the crowd. The hockey players form a loose circle around Elsy and—I blink—Anastasia, who looks radiant in an emerald gown. Beside her is a stunning blond woman in a red silk dress.

"Oh. It's you," Anastasia says, her lip curling in distaste at the sight of me.

I laugh, handing Elsy her drink. "Yep. I'm back."

She sighs. "Wonderful."

"It's almost time for our performance," Elsy says. "Do you mind keeping Katrina company?"

The blond waves. "Hi. I'm Katrina."

"Wyatt. Nice to meet you."

"So you're a symphony spouse, too, huh?" she comments.

My insides tighten. "Something like that."

"Well, we'll be spending a lot of time together, then," Katrina says. She kisses Anastasia. "Have an excellent performance. Break a leg. I'll be waiting for you when you're done."

I waggle my eyebrows at Elsy. "Want a kiss for good luck?"

She rolls her eyes. "Fuck off, Wyatt."

My heart thumps loudly. She loves me. She's *totally* in love with me.

eleven

· · ·

Elsy

THERE'S NOTHING ON TV, I don't have any friends in town, and I don't know what to do with my time. When I'm busy, it's easier to push the anxious thoughts to the back of my brain, but the second I have nothing else going on, they all come rushing in. The longer I go without a break, the stronger they attack. It's why I keep myself busy from the moment I wake until I'm ready for bed. Allowing myself down time allows me to spiral.

Anxiety is my nemesis as much as it's a comfort. I'm intimately familiar with the way my brain ruminates on every possible way life can go wrong. No matter what it is—a car ride across town, a performance in front of a packed hall, the idea of dating again—the dark thoughts settle me as much as they set me off. I know my patterns.

Is it healthy? No. Am I going to do something about it? Also no.

This morning, I met with two prospective students. One signed on to work with me, but the other is still mulling it over. After rehearsal, I ran a few errands and then came back to my cold, lonely apartment. I can't believe it, but I actually miss having roommates. There was always someone around to entertain me.

Anastasia and Katrina are out of town, enjoying a quick getaway for their anniversary. And I haven't connected with anyone else yet, not on the level where I'd be comfortable asking them to dinner or to grab coffee.

Well, that's not entirely true… I *do* know someone who's always around. With a sigh, I pick up my phone to text Wyatt. I don't want to do this. Especially after he witnessed my epic meltdown last week, I don't want to go to him again.

He promised to look out for me, after all. And as patronizing as it is… I kind of like the idea of someone taking care of me. Only a little bit. Not coddling, only… supporting.

Pulling up his contact, I stare at his name. Can I really do this? Is it worth putting myself out there? What if he says no? What if he mocks me for the rest of eternity?

Blowing out a breath, I click on his name, and my phone rings out with a dial tone. The call connects on the second ring.

"Elsy?" His voice is hoarse, the roughness sending heat rushing through me. That night… his *just been fucked* voice sounds a lot like this. "What's wrong?"

"Nothing's wrong." I pick at a loose thread on my throw blanket.

"You're calling me. Something's wrong."

This was a mistake.

"It was an accident. I'm hanging up now."

But I don't move the phone away from my ear.

His throaty chuckle does funny things to my heart rate. "No, you're not," he says, his voice soft, with an undercurrent of authority that makes my stomach clench.

"No, I'm not," I agree.

A rustle sounds on the other end. "So what's going on?"

My face heats. "I'm bored," I finally admit. "Do you want to do something?"

My heart pounds like I've run a marathon. Anxiety spikes within me, but it's not a panic attack, only run-of-the-mill worry. I don't think I can handle it if he says no. I know he's going to mock me for this.

"I'm in Dallas," Wyatt says. It almost sounds like he's upset about that. "I get back tomorrow morning. Do you…" He clears his throat. "Would you like to hang out tomorrow?"

"I can do that," I whisper.

"Great," he says. "I'm looking forward to it."

"Whoa. I wouldn't go that far." I laugh. "It's only hanging out. Don't propose or anything."

"Elsy," he says, his voice low and gravelly. "When I propose, it won't be a surprise."

My stomach swoops. He said *when*. Not *if*. What does that mean? We're not dating. We're not anything. In fact, I hate him. Does that mean he's thought about proposing to *me*, though?

No. That's ridiculous. He can't stand me, just like I can't stand him. He must be talking about a girlfriend.

"Are you dating anyone?"

He coughs. "Yeah, her name is hockey," he says. I can hear the smile in his voice.

"Oh."

"It's kind of hard to have an actual relationship when I'm on the road so much." He sounds… regretful. "I haven't tried it in a few seasons. I usually stick to a friends-with-benefits situation."

"Oh." I don't know how to respond to that.

"Why, are you offering?" He laughs, like the idea is so ludicrous, he can't possibly imagine it.

"Don't be ridiculous," I snap. "You and I are never going to sleep together."

Not again. I won't let myself be hurt that way ever again.

Silence falls over the line, the sound of his breathing steady and sure. It should be awkward, but it's not. It's strangely comforting knowing he's on the other end of the phone.

"Do you… want to talk about it?"

"Talk about what?"

"The other night." Wyatt clears his throat. "The panic attack."

"It happens sometimes." I pick at the loose thread again. I feel like I'm this close to unraveling myself. "Thanks for… you know."

"Have you seen someone about them?"

"Yeah. I take daily meds for it." Somehow, it doesn't feel weird talking about this. Vulnerable, yeah. Usually, I want to lock it up in a box and throw away the key. Knowing Wyatt's struggled with panic attacks of his own… for some reason, it makes me feel like I can trust him with this.

"Do you have rescue meds?"

"They make me crash. I think the dosage is too high. I'm trying to get established with a psychiatrist here." I exhale slowly. "If it didn't happen at work, I would have taken the meds. But I didn't think it would be a good idea to pass out on the stage. That would have made things worse."

I made it through my performance, but as soon as I got the go ahead from Hilary, I hightailed it out of there.

His deep chuckle sends tingles through my bloodstream. "I feel that. We have smelling salts on the bench. It's not the same, but it does help me focus."

"Maybe that's what I need."

"I'll grab some for you," he says.

"Oh, you don't have to do that."

"It's the least I can do. We have them everywhere."

I swallow. The unexpected offer feels… nice. Like he really is looking out for me. And not because Bex asked him to.

"Why are you being so nice to me?" I whisper.

Wyatt is quiet for a moment. "I'm just being me," he finally says.

"No. You're different lately."

"Elsy, I'm just being myself. You haven't been able to see it, but I haven't changed. I'm still the same me I've always been."

Right. He hasn't changed. He's still the same insensitive asshole he was all those years ago.

When I don't say anything, he asks, "Why'd you call me?"

"I told you. I was bored." A chill runs over me, making my skin rise in goose bumps. Why *did* I call him?

"Yeah. But why'd you call *me*?"

"I don't know."

He exhales slowly. "Okay. But when you figure it out, you let me know, okay?"

"Yeah, sure." I roll my eyes even though he can't see it. "What are you up to?"

"Just hanging at the hotel. I'm supposed to be taking my pregame nap."

"Oh. I'm bothering you. I should go." I don't know why I even called him.

"You're not a bother," Wyatt says. "I… like this."

"Don't make this weird," I snap at him. "It doesn't mean anything."

He laughs, sending a wave of warmth through me. "Yeah, okay."

"Have you talked to Bex recently?" I shift on the couch, stretching my legs out in front of me.

"Not in a few days."

"We talked last night. She's doing well."

"Good. I'm glad." His voice is warm and familiar, lulling me into complacency. "I worry about her."

"She's a grown woman. She can take care of herself."

"Yeah, but that doesn't mean I don't worry. Sometimes it's the strongest people who don't know how to take care of themselves. They're go, go, go all the time, they don't know how to rest. Or how to decompress. They put all their effort into being strong, so when they start to splinter, they fall apart and don't know how to pick up the pieces."

"What about you? Are you strong?"

"In some respects." He pauses. "I'm careful about taking breaks. I check in with my therapist regularly. It's hard with the demands of the season, but I take time off during the offseason and that goes a long way to helping me recharge. Resting on off days."

"Oh. You're off tomorrow. Does that mean you don't want to hang out? You need to rest." I bite my lip. Now that I've had some time to think about the idea, I don't hate it as much as I thought I would.

"I'll pick you up at noon. We'll go to lunch and see where the day goes from there."

I swallow. "Okay."

Everything about this conversation makes me uncomfortable, but in a good way, like I'm stretching muscles I haven't used in a while. I'm not used to feeling uncertain. I know who I am and what I want.

After everything with Stephen, I started to doubt myself.

No more. I won't let that continue. Wyatt might be confusing me, but I honestly don't think he's trying to mess with my head. He's a dick, yeah. But not cruel. Just an average asshole who says stupid things.

But if he spouts off about me to his buddies… That's it. The gloves are coming off. No more Miss Nice Girl.

A knock raps on my door, startling me from my thoughts, and with a sigh, I rise from the couch and hurry to the door.

"I should go. I have—"

The words die on my lips once I'm face-to-face with a stranger. Not my cute neighbor. "Delivery for Elsy Alexander," the guy says, holding out a bag of takeout.

Blinking, I take it. "I didn't order anything."

He shrugs. "I'm just delivering. Already paid for. Have a good day."

Hmm. Bex must have ordered me something. Or maybe Mitch. He does that kind of thing.

"What it is?" Wyatt asks in my ear, sounding smug.

"I'm not sure." Padding over to the counter and setting the phone down, I unbox the unexpected delivery.

There's a tuna sandwich on a croissant, a pint of potato salad, and three whole pickles.

"It's from the deli."

"Hmm. Imagine that," he says causally. Much too casually.

My eyes narrow at the phone, even though he can't see it. "Wyatt Whitney, did you send me food?"

"You sounded hungry," he says. I can practically hear him shrugging. "Can't have you wasting away on me."

"Thanks," I say. "You didn't have to do that."

"I wanted to."

Another protracted silence stretches between us. I don't know what to say.

"I'll pick you up at noon tomorrow," Wyatt finally says.

"Tomorrow," I repeat. A little thrill runs through me at the thought, equal parts nervous and excited.

"See you then."

twelve

. . .

Wyatt

ELSY IS WEARING A FUCKING SUNDRESS. It's like she knows they're my kryptonite. She's standing on the sidewalk in front of her apartment building, wearing a royal-blue sundress with a white halter strap around her neck, drawing my attention to her chest. The dress flows over her generous curves, making my cock twitch in my jeans.

Fuck. Why is she so fucking hot?

As I pull up to the curb, she breaks into a smile. I open my door, ready to get out and open hers, but she's already wrenching the door handle and sliding in beside me. I catch another hint of lace on her thighs and swallow, forcing my eyes onto the road ahead.

"Hey. How was your trip?" she asks.

"Good. We won." I managed an assist on Puppy's first NHL goal. That's something I'll carry with me. The kid has skills. It's clear he'll go far. One day, my name will be in the history books for that assist.

"I saw." She looks at me from the corner of her eye before she slips on her sunglasses. "Where are we going?"

"Lunch, first. Viggy recommended this place downtown,"

I tell her as I pull into traffic. "Then we'll figure it out from there."

"Sounds good."

We're quiet on the ride to the restaurant, but it's not awkward. I'm not sure what I expected after her unprompted phone call. I'm glad she called me, though. She reached out. *She* initiated. Maybe she doesn't hate me as much as I thought.

Or as much as she thought.

When we get to the restaurant, I'm quick to throw the car in park and get to her door before she can. My mother always taught me to open the door for a woman. It irritates me she doesn't let me do that for her.

Elsy gives me a strange look as I hold open her car door. "You don't have to do that."

"Do what?" I play dumb.

"You don't have to open my door. I'm perfectly capable of doing it myself."

"I know you are. I just want to."

She hums, clearly unimpressed.

"Let me do this," I tell her, keeping my voice soft and gentle. She's like a kitten; one sharp word, and she'll spook, and I'll lose the headway we've made lately. "It's important to me."

"Okay," she says after a moment. "What's next, you're going to pull out my chair and tell me I'm pretty?"

"You're very pretty." I set my hand on the small of her back as I guide her to the restaurant.

A beautiful shade of pink colors her cheeks. "You don't have to lie to me. Don't be a dick, Wyatt."

I stop in the middle of the entryway. Spinning her to face me, I set my hands on her shoulders, left bare by her dress straps.

"Elsy," I say seriously. "You are very pretty."

She swallows, and her eyes turn glassy, like she's about to cry.

I squeeze her shoulders. "You are beautiful. And it kills me that you can't let yourself believe that."

Her lower lip trembles. "Wyatt…"

"Friends don't let friends look down on themselves."

"Is that what we are?" she whispers. "Friends?"

"Well, I'd rather that than enemies."

She cocks her head, looking up at me for a long moment. Finally, she says, "I guess we can be friends."

"Good. Great."

So why am I disappointed?

Pushing down the confusing feelings welling within me, I slide my arm over Elsy's shoulders and lead her to the host's stand.

"Reservation for Whitney, please."

The hostess, who looks like she's barely eighteen, nods. "Right this way."

Elsy's hand darts out and grasps my arm. "This place is nice."

"Is it?"

Her grip tightens. "It's fancy. Why did you bring me here? Shit. Am I dressed okay?"

"You look great," I promise her. "Relax. The food's supposed to be good. If it sucks, we can leave and go to O'Malley's or whatever."

"Yeah. Okay. That works."

The hostess leads us over to a table by the window overlooking the river. The menu prices are a little much for lunch, but Viggy promised me the food was good, so I'll roll with it.

Elsy doesn't look thrilled, though.

"Wyatt, these prices…" She swallows. "I can't afford this."

She doesn't like to admit weakness, in any respect. And now for her to be so frank…

"I've got it. It's my treat."

She frowns.

"If you don't want to eat here, we don't have to. If you want to stay, though, it's on me."

Hesitation crosses her face. "I don't know…"

"I can afford to buy you lunch ten times over, and I won't even blink. I would never force you to do something you didn't want to do. But don't let money keep you from enjoying something that could be great."

"Yeah, you can say that. You have piles of money." Her bitter laugh makes my chest ache. I hate that she's so resentful of something neither of us can control.

"I didn't always," I remind her. "I'm lucky to be able to play the sport that I love, but I'm well aware it can all go away in the blink of an eye. One bad play, one big hit, and I could be out of the game forever. I put my body on the line every day."

Elsy stares at me. If she's surprised by any of this, I can't tell. Her best friend playing in the league doesn't mean she knows all the ins and outs of the actual reality of the lifestyle.

"My knees are shot, my shoulder is fucked, and let's not even talk about how many times I've broken my nose."

Four times, including once because of her. Half of my teeth are implants, too. But that's not sexy, so I'm not going to bring it up.

"The reality of playing hockey is very different from the glamorous lifestyle you see online. It's hard work."

"I know it's hard work," she murmurs. "I'm not disputing that."

"Okay. So what's the issue?"

Her lips form a thin line. "It just sucks that I can barely pay my bills and have to take a second job to play music, and you get millions of dollars thrown your way for chasing a puck around."

"It does suck," I agree, and I think that surprises her,

because her face gets this adorably pinched look. "It's absolutely not fair. If I knew how to fix it, I would."

I donated to the symphony the night of the gala. Some guys bid for items in the silent auction. Henry quietly made a donation, too. I only know because I saw him stuff a check into the bin. He might act like a sleazy playboy, but I think there might be more substance to him buried inside—deep, *deep* inside.

Elsy is quiet, gazing at me. It's like she can see right inside me, into my soul. It should be uncomfortable. With anyone else, I'd be cracking a joke to break the tension. Except there's no tension.

With her? I'm content to sit here and look at her, and her look at me. I feel calm and at peace in a way I don't experience with other people. Even my parents stress me out. Only Bex can set me at ease this way.

Does that mean I want Elsy to be my sister?

The immediate revulsion ricocheting through me is answer enough. Elsy is *not* my sister and I definitely don't feel that way about her.

She's hot. I've wanted to sleep with her again ever since that first time. Is that all this is?

The waiter interrupts my tumultuous thoughts. He runs through the specials, then takes our drink orders. Elsy orders a Coke, so I do, too. I don't need to drink alcohol every time I'm around her. In fact, it's probably better if I don't. I need to keep my wits about me when it comes to her.

She's dangerous to be around. I just don't know if that's a good thing yet.

"How are rehearsals going?" There, that should be a natural topic.

"Good. I'm keeping up with the repertoire," Elsy says, settling into her seat. "Anastasia and I have gotten together a few times."

"And she's your competition?" I don't really understand

how the first chair/second chair thing works, only that she used to be first back in Boston and now she isn't.

"Technically, yes," she says. "Right now, I'm still getting settled. Eventually, I'll try to move up. If it happens, it happens. And if it doesn't..." She blows out a breath. "I'm trying to take it one day at a time and not plan everything out ten years into the future."

"Oh?"

"Yeah. I'm kind of a planning nut." She gives me a self-deprecating smile. "My anxiety is soothed by knowing what's going to happen and when, and if something deviates from the plan, it tends to worsen the symptoms."

"That makes sense. My anxiety is more, what if I let the team down, what if I get injured, what if this is my last game and I don't know it," I tell her. "Then I start spiraling into how I'm a disappointment and not worthy of everything I've achieved, and, well, I call it the dark place and I try to avoid it as much as possible."

Elsy frowns. "You're not a disappointment, Wyatt."

My laugh is bitter. "I'm a college dropout."

"So?"

"So my dad is a doctor, my mom is a lawyer, and my sister has her PhD before she's thirty." Frustration lodges itself deep in my chest, behind my ribcage, and I rub the ache, trying to clear it away. It doesn't work. "I'm not diminishing the work it took to get to the NHL. I recognize that I'm lucky. But I can also recognize that in my family and within their friend groups, I'm nothing but a hotheaded college dropout with no career prospects once hockey dries up."

My breathing is coming a little faster now. I'm not angry, not at her. At my family, yes. At my circumstances. At the world.

But I could never be angry with Elsy. I don't think I have it in me.

She reaches across the table, grabbing hold of my hand.

My skin lights up at her touch. Flipping my hand over, she sets her palm on mine, squeezing my fingers.

"Wyatt, you are an incredible hockey player," she says, her eyes locked on mine. "But that's not all you are. I'll have to prove it to you."

"How are you going to do that?" My voice comes out in a croak.

"I'm not sure yet," she admits. "If you need me to, I will."

I think I need her to. But I don't know how to ask for that.

Fuck. Guess I better book in for another session with my therapist. Probably wouldn't hurt to connect with my sports psychologist, too.

Clearing my throat, I try to recalibrate. I should say something here. I need to change the subject. What do I say?

I'm saved by the waiter arriving with our food. Elsy pulls away. Am I imagining the reluctance on her face?

The food is as good as I was led to believe, and from the way Elsy digs into her entrée, she seems to agree. The blissed-out expression on her face when she drags her salmon through the chimichurri sauce makes my pants inexplicably tight.

She talks about her students and the upcoming performances with the symphony. I mention my upcoming games. It's all very surface level, a welcome relief after the earlier heaviness.

And as we walk out of the restaurant and I set my hand on the small of her back, she smiles up at me, and maybe, just maybe, I wonder if this could be the start of something new for us.

thirteen

. . .

Elsy

AFTER LUNCH, Wyatt drove us out to Lady Bird Lake. We walked a lap around the lake before he convinced me to take out one of the paddleboats.

Turns out, my propensity for carsickness extends to boats, so we quickly ended that adventure.

Instead, we got *paletas* from a nearby vendor with a push-cart full of popsicles and sat on a park bench for two hours. It didn't feel like it was all that long at the time.

When he dropped me off at my apartment at the end of the afternoon, I was surprisingly energized for having spent a day with someone else. Usually, spending time with people is a drain on my energy, no matter how much I love them. Even Bex and Mitch drive me nuts after a few hours, and I need some time to decompress.

But with Wyatt... I don't feel that need. In fact, I almost invited him up to hang out more until he said something about hitting the gym and I noped out of there.

Instead, I cleaned my apartment, did two loads of laundry, and read a book cover to cover. Now all that's done with and I'm... lonely.

I'm lonely.

By nature, I'm a homebody. I like to be at my apartment, and I like to be myself, and I don't think those are bad things. While I'm perfectly capable of entertaining myself—with a good book, with crochet, watching a movie, making a home-made spa day—I've never felt the need to be around someone else all the time.

Plus, I've always had roommates before. This is the first time I'm not living with anyone else. To my surprise, I kind of miss it. It was nice knowing I could venture out of my room and Bex or Vanessa would be there to chat or watch a movie together. I always knew I could text any of the twenty girls in our book club and someone would be down to grab dinner or drinks.

I'm used to having a social network. And now I don't.

After the symphony chose to keep my cheating, emotion-ally manipulative ex and dumped me to "keep the peace," I'm not about to double-dip with the symphony, not again. I've learned my lesson, thank you very much.

Having moved crisscross the country a few times, I've always known someone in my city or had a reason for being there. College, everyone was new. Then grad school, we were all working for the same degree. Or my first job in Chicago, close to where my cousins lived. And in Boston, I had Bex, who introduced me to her friend group, where they welcomed me with open arms.

My social media is pretty locked down. Between the symphony and my being associated with Mitch, I'm a private person who is tangentially connected to the spotlight. There have been plenty of people over the years who have tried to use me to get ahead. Now I only accept friends I know in person to have access to my profile.

But I'll never make real-life friends here in town if I don't try.

So I type out a public post, looking for women in their thirties who like romance books and watching hockey. And then I set the location to Austin and click submit.

Stuffing my phone into my bra, I'm determined not to look at it. Instead, I vacuum the living room and dust the bookshelves. I make a pot of Kraft mac and cheese for dinner because I'm still a kid at heart, even if my driver's license says otherwise.

But then my phone buzzes. Pulling it out of my boob pocket, I blink at the screen in surprise. There are seven comments on my post in the first ten minutes.

Laughing to myself, I start to tap out replies. Maybe this will work. I'm not going to get my hopes up, not yet. I still have to meet these internet strangers to figure out if they're serial killers or not. Let's hope not.

This could be the start of something new.

———

Wyatt has two back-to-back games, first against Anaheim, then Edmonton. I have a performance on the night of the first game so I make a point to attend the second. I'm not sure why it's so important to me that I'm there, but I guess he is my only friend here until my new online friends can meet in person. And I'm *definitely* not inviting them to come watch a game until I can be sure they won't freak out at the idea of hanging out with a professional hockey player.

Anyone else would kill for my usual seat behind the bench, so close I can practically see the sweat drip down the back of the players' necks. Even after spending the better part of the last decade around the league, the electricity that floods my veins when the puck drops doesn't get old.

During pregame skate, Wyatt grinned at me and waved, and Henry flipped me a puck. I gave it to the kid a few rows behind me, which made her day, and which made Henry shake his head. But he was smiling, so I don't think he was too upset.

The generic Aces jacket I bought myself barely wards off the chill from the ice, and I clutch it tighter around me to try to find a bit more warmth. I'm sure if I asked, Wyatt would get me his jersey, but that's crossing a line. The only guy's name I've ever worn is Mitch's. It's not romantic in the slightest. I love him like a brother. Even with the Grizzlies, I never wore any specific player's number. Though knowing the guys in person made them less appealing.

Hockey players don't do it for me. But how much of that is because of the way Wyatt spoke about me to his hockey buddies? I was certainly attracted to him that night…

Not to mention the other day at the lake, when I saw a different side of Wyatt—one I'd never experienced before. If he wasn't needling me, he was always politely distant. That day, it was like he actually wanted to know what I was thinking. He cared about what I had to say.

We talked about my parents splitting up, about the demands his put on him. I told him things I've never told anyone, not even Mitch. It wasn't scary. It felt… natural.

And now, sitting in the stands to watch his game, I'm second-guessing all of that. There's no way that nice, charming man is the same guy who allowed his buddies to talk shit about me, then followed it up with *hey, at least I got laid.*

All I got was thirteen years of poor self-esteem and self-doubt.

I thought I was past it when I started up with Stephen. I was a grown adult, mature, ready to tackle my issues head-on.

And then when he dumped me, telling me I was so bad in bed, he couldn't pretend to like me anymore… well, all of that came crashing back.

I had to take a hard look at myself in the mirror. I refuse to be swayed by the taunts of small-minded men. He won't get to me.

Which means I can't let Wyatt get to me, either. Whatever games he's trying to play, I won't be part of it. No, it's best to put a little more distance between us. We're not friends, not really.

The rookie, Riley, pots a goal in the net off Wyatt's assist, and I almost swear Wyatt is looking for me in the crowd as he zooms past the bench for their post-goal celly. His expression clears when we make eye contact, and he winks at me.

My entire body warms, and my insides sizzle with aware-ness. It must be from the body heat of everyone around me.

Sitting back in my seat, I take a few photos and send them to Bex and the girls from my book club back in Boston. Just because I've moved to a new city doesn't mean I don't still think about them. The girls won't get rid of me that easily.

At the intermission, I head up to the concourse to grab a snack. Watching hockey is hungry work, and as I've learned over the last few weeks, the food at the Austin Arena is particularly ace.

It's packed with sweaty, smelly bodies, as if the fans have been sweating in their seats as much as the players on the ice. As I'm surrounded by a swarm of navy and gold jerseys in the bathroom line, my phone buzzes in my pocket.

It's Wyatt.

Meet me after the game.

A body crashes into me, jostling my hand. The autocorrect picks up ghostlike movements, and a string of nonsensical words appear on the screen before I accidentally hit send.

snake wrote is your dinner home

The dancing dots of Wyatt's reply taunt me. What's he going to say?

Don't stroke out on me, Elsy. Not yet.

Do I do this?

fourteen

. . .

Wyatt

"DUDE," Henry says after the game.

I roll my eyes. "What?"

"She's here."

"Who?"

He pins me with a flat look. "Your girl."

Heat fills my cheeks, and it has nothing to do with the vigorous game we played. "She's not my girl."

Except after our afternoon together, I went home and started thinking. Elsy asked me, during the phone call *she* initiated, if I was dating someone. Is that her angling for something? She willingly spent the whole day with me, and we sat on that park bench for two hours talking. And I don't do that with just anyone. Hell, I can't think of a time I've *ever* done that before.

That day... it was fun. I didn't have to think too hard. I didn't have to force myself to have fun. It happened without trying.

When she's not throwing barbs at me, I enjoy hanging around with Elsy. Fuck, even when she's eviscerating me, I like to be around her.

"She's looking good out there," Henry comments as he strips off his gear.

"Fuck off."

I won't let him needle me. He's an expert at it, exactly like I am. He knows how to get under my skin. But I won't let him.

"I'm just saying." Henry shrugs. "If she's not your girl, you won't mind if I ask her out, then?"

My stomach twists at the idea of Elsy and Henry. She deserves better than a sleazy playboy with pucks for brains.

And what if she falls for him? And it's all a game to him?

A throaty growl rumbles through me. We've had this conversation before. I thought I warned him off enough. Clearly, I need to make sure everyone in this goddamn arena knows she's off-limits.

Henry punches my shoulder. "If she's not your girl, you better fix that, and fast. Otherwise someone else will swoop in and snatch her up. I'm guessing that dude won't give you a heads-up."

"She can date whoever she wants," I grind out.

"Yeah, but you want it to be you."

I blink. Do I? She's fucking gorgeous, but as much as I like her, am I ready for dating and everything that comes with it? Can I handle a real, grown-up relationship, the kind that lasts forever?

Clarity settles in the pit of my stomach, wafting over me like the smelling salts we use to get our head in the game. I want to date Elsy.

Fuck. I want to date *Elsy*.

She hates me—and rightfully so, considering what a dick I was. How can I prove to her I'm not that insecure kid anymore? How can I convince her to give me another chance?

Elsy is waiting in the friends and family hallway. As I approach with Henry and Puppy trailing behind me, she gives me a radiant smile, her eyes bright.

"Good game," she says, her eyes flicking behind me as if she's dismissing me already.

Am I invisible to her? Or is she more interested in my teammates than she is in me? Either way, it stings, and I rub my chest like it will make the ache go away.

"Congrats on the goal."

Puppy puffs up his chest. "Thanks."

He scored another tonight, bringing his tally to three in six games. Not a terrible start for a rookie on the fourth line with limited minutes. One of these days, he's going to get bumped up to the third line with more playing time.

Then again, the three of us play fairly well together, so maybe they'll keep us on the same line after all.

"There's this new club downtown I've been meaning to check out," Henry says casually. He gives me a pointed look. I can't tell if he's goading me or encouraging me. Maybe both. "You want to come?"

I hesitate. The last thing I want to do is be at a club until ass o'clock in the morning and nurse a hangover all through our early practice tomorrow.

"Can I come?" Riley asks.

"Sure, Pup," Henry says, and he scowls.

"Fuck off," he mutters, but he doesn't sound angry at the nickname. In fact, he almost sounds pleased.

"How about it?" I turn to Elsy. "You in?"

She pauses. "I don't know. Am I dressed okay?"

Well, if she's asking... I trail my gaze over her thick curves, her tight jeans and sneakers, drinking in the sight of her. She's wearing an Aces zip-up—not the kind with a guy's number on the back, but a generic team jacket.

"Yeah, you look great," I tell her honestly.

She bites her lip. "Most of these clubs have a dress code..."

And we're all wearing our post-game suits.

"Don't worry about it," Henry says. "If you're with us, you'll get in."

Elsy gives him a skeptical look.

Teasingly, I nudge her with my elbow. "You forget the draw of hockey players."

But she doesn't laugh. Instead, she almost looks sad. "I guess so."

I slip my arm around her shoulders, and when she doesn't shrug me off, I count it as a victory. "Come on, I'll drive."

Her brow furrows. "I'm not driving your car when you get stupid drunk. We should call an Uber."

"I won't get wasted," I promise her.

I can't look out for her if I'm drinking heavily. One, maybe two. That's all I'll have. I know my limits.

———

The bouncer lets us in with no problem. He didn't even glance at Elsy, busy scrutinizing Puppy more closely before stamping his hand as under twenty-one. The rookie doesn't seem to mind, too excited to be out with us. We left our suit jackets in the car and I took my time rolling up my shirtsleeves, noticing how Elsy kept sneaking peeks out of the corner of her eye. I don't understand women's obsession with forearms, but hey, I'll do whatever I can to get her attention on me.

"I'll grab drinks," I offer.

Henry raises an eyebrow. My eyes narrow, flicking to Elsy, who's vibing to the beat. We have a silent conversation with our eyes, a jerk of my chin, and he shrugs, before he sighs and nods. He'll look out for her.

He may be a sleazy playboy, but he's a good dude. Most of the time. He certainly seems to care about her, though I've never seen him care about anyone else before.

"Els, you drinking?" Henry asks.

"Just one." Her eyes dart between him and me. "Tito's and—"

"Tito's and Sprite. I've got you." I know all of her favorites. She's a creature of habit, just like me. We like our structure, our routines.

And she's sending mine all wonky.

Henry says something to her, something I can't hear. Evidently, she can't either, because he leans down and speaks into her ear. She nods, and then he's grabbing her hand, pulling her into the throng of people on the dance floor.

"So, like," Riley says. "Is this some kind of sharing thing? Because I've heard rumors in the locker room…"

"Fuck off. No, you haven't."

"Because I thought you two were together, but now they're out on the dance floor, and—"

"We're not together," I grit out. Spinning on my heels, I stalk off toward the bar, and he follows close behind me.

"So why is she always hanging around?" Riley is like a dog with a bone.

"Because she wants to."

"She a puck bunny?"

Whirling around to face him, I glare at the rookie with all the ferocity of my nine years in the league as a brawler. "You keep your filthy hands off of her."

But Puppy is grinning, raising his hands to profess his innocence. "Just trying to figure out what's going on. I would never go after your girl."

That's what he said at the gala, too. I still wouldn't put it past him.

"She's not my girl," I repeat.

The kid rolls his eyes. "Yeah, I figured, if you let Henry put his paws all over her."

Unease runs through me. I don't like the constant reminders that Henry gets to have her in a way I don't. She's *nice* to him. Even with the fragile friendship we have now, she's still holding back.

"Fuck off."

We make it to the front of the bar, and I order Elsy's drink plus two beers, and Puppy gets a Coke. The bartender eyes us curiously, but I have no intention of giving an underage kid alcohol. Not when it could end his career. He has too much potential.

Drinks in hand, we push and shove our way to the dance floor. Henry has his hands on Elsy's hips as they dance together. Her arms are around his neck, but there's a good buffer of space between their torsos.

A growl rumbles through me, vibrating in my bones. *She's mine.* I mean, she's not *mine*, but she's certainly not *his*.

I don't care that he's watching out for her, keeping the other lecherous dudes in the club away. If we hadn't had the conversation in the locker room, I don't know I'd even let him get this close.

Shaking the thought away, I focus on the happiness on her face. If I can't trust my linemate, who else can I trust?

She's lost herself to the music, her hips swaying to the beat, her head tossed back. Her blond ponytail shakes as she shimmies.

Henry's eyes meet mine and he gives me a nod as I approach, handing him his beer.

I set my newly freed hand on her hip, and she whirls around like she's about to punch me out.

But when she sees it's me, she relaxes. I offer her the drink and she takes a sip, her eyes fluttering shut.

Fuck. I remember seeing that expression of bliss on her face when my fingers were deep within her pussy. And again when she came on my tongue. And then with my cock buried in her…

Slipping behind her, I press my front to her back, trying to find a rhythm. Elsy lets her head fall back against my shoulder, her arm still around Henry's neck.

That won't do. I draw her arm back, to hook it behind my neck, and he responds by moving closer, nudging his leg between her thick thighs.

Elsy's eyes dart between us. "Okay, what's going on?"

"What do you mean?" I duck my head to speak directly into her ear.

"Is this some kind of freaky threesome thing?"

My stomach lurches as my entire body shudders with revulsion.

No.

No, I don't like the idea of sharing her. I don't care who else is involved, I only want it to be me and her. Nobody else.

"We're not going to have a threesome," I growl.

"Because we're not going to sleep together," she says, equally resolute. "If you guys want to find someone else to be the meat in your sandwich, go ahead. It won't be me."

Through it all, Henry is right there, dancing against her. But there's a considerable buffer between them, whereas she's pressed right up against my chest. I've lost track of Puppy in the fray, but I'm confident he can handle himself.

"Do you want me to get him to leave?" I ask Elsy.

"I just want to know what this is."

"We're dancing." I swivel my hips against her ass, my hand trailing up her flank to her ribs, then back to her hip. "Isn't that what you wanted?"

"I—I—"

Pinching her chin between two fingers, I meet her gaze. "What is it you want, Elsy?"

fifteen

. . .

Elsy

BEFORE I KNOW what's come over me, I rise onto my toes and kiss him. He tastes like the beer he's been sipping, with an undercurrent of fresh mint and something familiar. It takes me back to that night all those years ago. And where that would usually make me sad or even angry, right now, I'm remembering the good.

Wyatt cups my cheek, deepening the kiss. His lips whisper against mine, telling me something I don't think I'm ready to hear.

One day, maybe one day soon, I'll be able to listen. But I'm not ready. I don't know if I ever will be. All I know is, there's a gorgeous guy kissing me back, and even though I think I hate him... I also think I don't. Hate him, that is.

Henry goes away, and I notice the loss only in the faraway corner of my brain. My entire focus narrows in on Wyatt and this moment, this kiss.

Fuck, can he kiss. Did I forget, or did I bury it in the far recesses of my mind?

Wyatt makes a soft noise into my mouth. He breaks the kiss, but he doesn't go far, resting his forehead on mine. His soft breaths puff against my lips, sending a shiver down my spine.

"I'm sorry," I say automatically.

"Don't be sorry," he says. "I've wanted to do that all night."

It's my turn to pull back. "What?"

He nods, meeting my eyes. "Ever since I saw you in the stands."

"Wyatt…"

He looks around at the crowded dance floor. "This isn't the place to talk. Do you want to keep talking, or do you want to dance?"

I pause.

I want to get to the bottom of this. What does it mean? Is he trying to hook up and bounce? Or, fuck, will he get me naked and then destroy me again?

But as I look at the serious, open expression on his face… I know I have to trust him. Trust myself.

"Let's dance."

He nods, pressing a soft kiss to the corner of my mouth before he sets his hand back on my hip. His thick, wide body presses against me from behind, crowding me in the best way. I'm surrounded by him, enveloped in his warm scent, citrus and clove and a little bit of musk. The familiarity of it is reassuring. Surrounded by hundreds of strangers, I know he's there to protect me.

A few weeks ago, I'd have laughed myself silly at the idea that Wyatt would ever look out for me. He doesn't give two shits about me. And maybe that was true then. But over the last few days, something has changed. I can't put my finger on it. I only know that the Wyatt I've gotten to know lately is different from the guy who could barely stand to look at me the day I moved here.

That guy never would have kissed me.

Or let me kiss him.

Why did I kiss him?

It's not the alcohol; I've barely had two sips of my drink. Something else must be wrong with me. Maybe it's a brain tumor.

Or maybe I simply wanted to. Does it have to be more than that?

Wyatt slips his hand from my hip to wrap his arm around my belly, hauling me back against him. "I'm doing some pretty good work here," he says low in my ear. "What's going on with you?"

He brushes his nose against my hair.

"I'm fine."

"You're stiff as a board." He's practically hugging me. "Do you not want this?"

Turning in the circle of his embrace, I spin to face him. He pulls my arms around his neck and slides his hands down my back until we're chest to chest. I can feel every inhalation he makes.

His icy blue eyes are locked on mine.

I want to kiss him again. I might even want to do more than that. But I won't do it on the dance floor of this seedy club.

"Elsy," he says, his voice rumbling through me. "What's going on?"

"Let's get out of here." My voice wavers and I swallow my fears. My eyes flick to his plush, kissable lips, then back up. "Take me home, Wyatt."

His eyes search mine urgently. "Els—"

"Take me home."

Withdrawing, he nods slowly. He offers me his hand and, when I take it, he laces our fingers together.

Tipping back his beer bottle, he drains it in one go, the thick column of his throat working as he swallows. Heat sizzles through me. I don't understand this unexpected attraction to him. It's completely out of nowhere.

Except it's not. He's been different lately. It just took me a while to catch up.

Once we're out of the club, the evening chill hits like a brick wall. I shiver and Wyatt draws me into his side, his arm draped around my shoulder to protect me from the brisk wind.

"Do you want to—"

"Shut up," I cut him off.

He falls silent, miming zipping his lips. When we get to the car, he unlocks my door for me to slide in, then hurries around to the driver's side. He always does that. Opens my door, that is. But I never noticed until he pointed it out.

What else have I missed?

Once he sets the car in drive, his hand falls off the gearshift to land on my knee. I set my hand on his and he looks over at me, sending me a happy smile.

"Yeah?"

Am I ready for more than a kiss? Am I ready to let my guard down, to truly let him in?

So I grab his hand, drawing it up to where I want him, high on my upper thigh. His fingers flex, gripping my flesh before he lets out a gusty sigh and relaxes.

I still don't know where I want the rest of the night to go. I'm not sure what I'm ready for.

The air in the car is thick with tension. I don't know what to say, what to do. It feels wrong to make small talk. Hey, you just had your tongue in my mouth, let's talk about the weather? Come on.

When we reach my apartment, he pulls into the visitor spot out front and cuts the engine before turning to face me.

"What do you want, Elsy?" His voice is as smooth as velvet, his eyes focused on mine. "Do you want me to walk you to your door? Or do you want to call it a night?"

He's putting himself out there. The least I can do is the same.

"I want you to come in," I finally say. My hands shake and I clasp them together to hide it. "I don't know what's going to happen, but…"

Wyatt swallows. "Okay. Yeah, I can do that."

Together, we exit the car. His hand finds mine so naturally, his thumb stroking the back of my knuckles as we walk through the building to my door.

It takes me three tries to get the key in the lock. His hand covers mine.

"Hey, it's okay," he murmurs. "Nothing has to happen that you don't want."

"I know," I snap. He can't force me to do anything I don't want to do. Not that I think he ever would. He might be an asshole, but he's not that way. He'd never push me past my limit or do anything without my explicit consent.

"And if you want me to leave, I can—"

"Don't." The word slips out before I can stop it, and I swallow my hesitation, my eyes flicking up to his. "Don't go."

Wyatt nods slowly. "Okay. I won't go."

He takes the key from me to unlock the door, holding it open for me. I probably should have picked up before I left for the game, but I wasn't exactly expecting company.

"Do you want to watch a movie?" he asks.

"Shut up, Wyatt."

"Shutting up."

Okay. Oxygen floods my lungs as I take a slow, deep, calming breath, steadying my nerves. I'm not sure what my limit is, but he seems game to play, so… Fake it until the confidence is real. I can do that.

As I press on his chest, he takes a step back, then another, until he lets me walk him over to the couch. The cushion dips as he sits automatically, and before I can regret it, I straddle his lap.

"Hi." My voice comes out hoarse.

"Hello." His smile is audible. "What do you want, Elsy?"

"Why do you keep asking me that?"

"Because I want to know." He runs a hand through the wispy tufts of hair that have fallen out of my ponytail. "I want to know everything about you."

Hesitantly, I wind my arms around his neck, and he lets out a soft sigh, adjusting my positioning until we're practically nose to nose. He darts forward and pecks my lips. A simple, quick kiss.

"Why?"

"Because I do." He gives a little shrug. "Why not?"

"Most people don't." I look away, but his hand on my cheek brings my focus back to him.

"I'm not most people."

"No, you're not."

His eyes search mine. There's a heaviness in his gaze, some deeper meaning I'm not sure of.

Carefully, he cups the back of my head, then brings his lips to mine. The kiss is soft. Tentative.

I don't want tentative.

Deepening the kiss, I sweep my tongue into his mouth, tasting him again. He fights me for control, but I stand my ground, not backing down. He's always so controlled, so careful. Just once I'd love to see what he's like when he lets go.

sixteen

. . .

Wyatt

ELSY DOESN'T GIVE me an inch and I fucking love it. Her fingers tiptoe over the column of my sternum, then down to my abs before I have to stop her.

It's with great reluctance that I pull my hands away from her.

"What do you want?" I ask again. "What can I give you?"

Is companionship all she's looking for? Does she want a hard, dirty fuck? Or does she want someone to make her feel wanted and appreciated?

Whatever it is, I'm down. Well, rather, *up*.

With her straddling my lap, I'm sure she can feel the hard length of my erection pressing against her ass. I'm not trying to make her uncomfortable, but I can't deny that this gorgeous woman straddling me is driving me crazy.

She reaches for the zip of her hoodie, drawing it down. I help her get it off, tossing it to the ground. Underneath, she's wearing a thin black tank top, which is doing a terrible job at keeping her tits contained. She's practically spilling out of her shirt. I have to force my gaze back to her face.

She doesn't look upset at my gawking, though. If

anything, she's almost amused. Does that mean I can look the way I've wanted to every day for the last thirteen years?

"They're great tits, aren't they?" she says, her lips curving into a smile.

"Yeah, they are."

And when she doesn't skewer me for looking, I bury my face in her chest, kissing the inner sides of her breasts.

Her amused laughter turns into a soft pant when I kiss and suck at her flesh, even with the thin cotton material in the way.

"Wyatt…" My name is a plea on her lips, making my hard cock twitch.

Pulling back, I cup her cheek. "Can I take it off?"

She hesitates.

"Please?"

After a moment, Elsy nods, her reluctance clear as day on her face.

"We don't have to do anything you don't want to do," I remind her.

"No, I just…" She turns red and looks away.

"Tell me."

"I don't like taking my shirt off in front of guys. It's not sexy."

Ice fills my veins. "You think you're not sexy?"

Has she looked in a fucking mirror lately? She's the hottest fucking woman on this goddamn planet.

Her face crumples. "Look, you don't have to lie to me. I know what I look like."

"Do you? Do you really?" Because if she saw even half of what I see when I look at her, she wouldn't be thinking like this. "You're gorgeous, Els. So fucking gorgeous."

She rolls her eyes. "You're ridiculous."

"You are a badass, rock-star musician. You moved halfway across the country, knowing nobody in this city, because you knew you needed to make a change. That's fucking badass."

"I'm going to need you to write those affirmations on the mirror, then," she jokes. Her smile falls. "I also have—"

"You have the best tits I've ever seen and an ass that won't quit." I grind my hard cock against her ass. If she won't listen, I'll show her.

Elsy scowls. "Yeah, but I also have this." She grabs the rolls of her belly.

"And? What's the problem?"

"It's not sexy." She lifts her chin like I won't hear the wobble in her voice.

"Babe, you have no fucking idea how sexy you are."

Her lip trembles. "But—"

"Let me show you."

Every inch of her fuck-hot body freezes.

"Please, Elsy? Can I show you?"

She gives me a quick nod, like she's afraid I'll change my mind if she waits too long. Not a chance of that happening. I've been waiting for this for thirteen fucking years.

Wrapping my arms around her, I stand with her twisted around me like a pretzel.

Elsy squeals. "Wyatt! Let me down."

"No. I've got a job to do."

"I'm too heavy. You'll get injured."

"You aren't, and I won't."

Walking into her bedroom, I kick the door closed behind us and turn on the bedside lamp. The mattress jostles as I drop her on the unmade bed. She's still wearing her sneakers. That won't do. I toe mine off, too.

Anticipation makes my mouth water as I drop to my knees beside the bed. I start with her feet, slipping off her shoes and setting them aside before peeling off her socks. She tries to spread her legs but I stay where I am. Taking her foot in my hand, I run my thumb up the arch. Elsy lets out a soft sigh, relaxing into my touch. I massage the tension out of the left foot, then the right, before trailing my fingers up her calves.

She tries to spread her legs again, and this time, I let her, climbing up onto the bed.

Her blond ponytail is loose, her hair splayed out on the pillow like an angel's halo, and her cheeks have a rosy flush, her chest rising and falling with quick, staccato breaths.

"Wyatt, I—"

When I reach her midsection, I glide the hem of her tank top up until her midriff is exposed. She tries to cover her belly with her arm, but I push it away.

"Let me see you." My voice comes out gravelly and hoarse.

She allows me to pull off her top and I'm treated to the wondrous sight of her tits in a lacy black bra.

"Can this come off?" I trace a line under her breasts, at the little divot in the center of her ribcage.

Elsy hesitates but then nods.

"You're in control. You tell me if you want me to stop."

Her chin juts out, petulant. "Did I fucking tell you to stop?"

"Well… no."

She reaches behind her and unsnaps her bra, tossing it to the floor. "So fucking carry on."

She's fucking gorgeous, her body on display for me. Greedy, I drink her in. I could get lost in her body, again and again.

But we only have tonight. If I only have one chance at this, I have to make it good for her. I have a job to do.

Before I can get distracted more, I reach for the button of her high-rise jeans, slowly lowering the zipper. I tug at the denim, getting it over her hips and down her thighs. Thick red lines crisscross her skin where the material has dug in. I kiss along the lines, over and over. My hands dig into her ass, kneading her cheeks.

She's wearing little satin panties. Baby blue.

Fuck.

I bring my nose to her pussy, inhaling her musky scent. She smells so good. I'm desperate for a taste, but I know I have to take care of her first. She's my priority.

My eyes flutter closed as I reach for the waistband of her underwear. Once she's naked before me, it takes everything in me to meet her gaze.

"Tell me you want this."

"I—I do."

I shake my head. "Elsy. Tell me you want this."

She glares at me. "If you don't fucking touch me—"

Running my thumb through her slit, I trace a featherlight circle around her clit.

"Like this?"

She lets out an aggravated groan. "I really don't like you right now."

As much as I want to take her comment at face value, I can't deny it stings. I want her to like me. I want her to love me.

Whoa. Where did that come from? Love? This is just sex. That's all it is.

Right?

"I don't have to do this. I can leave." I dip my finger lower, putting pressure against her entrance without pressing inside. "Just tell me to go."

Elsy props herself up onto her elbows, a scowl on her face. "Put your fucking finger inside of me." A wicked grin paints my lips.

Well, if the lady asks so nicely…

Twisting my wrist, I slip a finger inside her tight, wet heat. Her pussy pulses around me and my neglected cock throbs in the confines of my suit pants.

But this isn't about me. This is about her.

Sinking lower in the bed, I kiss the lines on the inside of

her thighs and the crease of her hip as my finger fucks slowly in and out. When she relaxes enough for me to slide a second finger in, I suck her clit into my mouth.

Her silky, velvety walls flutter around my fingers. And when her hips roll against my mouth, drawing my fingers deeper inside of her as she rides me, my balls draw up high and tight, desperate for release.

She looks so beautiful, her face awash in pleasure. Elsy slides her hands into my hair, gripping the strands tight. She isn't afraid to take what she needs and I'm more than happy to give it to her, for her to use my body for her own needs. Any part of me, it's all hers.

My cock throbs, and I press my pelvis into the mattress, seeking enough relief to let me concentrate. Her scent and her sounds and her taste have me on the edge. I'm a live wire, every nerve ending electrified by her.

I focus on her, on the angles that make her moan and the pressure that makes her clench around my fingers. Most of all, I pay attention to *her*.

Her eyes are closed, her face relaxed as she lets me bring her satisfaction. My free hand touches everywhere—her breasts, pinching her nipples; cupping her ass; stroking her arm. And I let my hand rove over her belly, over the rolls she says she hates but drive me crazy, over the curves and indentations of her body.

She's absolutely fucking perfect, just the way she is. I wouldn't care if she weighed a hundred pounds less or a hundred pounds more; she would still be so fucking sexy, no matter the shape of her body. The *inside* of her body is what draws me to her, the sensitive soul and the smart brain and the quick wit. Her kindness. Her joy.

It's her.

My cock jerks in my suit pants and it takes everything in me not to shove my free hand into my pants for some relief. This isn't about me. It's about her.

It's always been about her.

Elsy tightens her grip in my hair, pulling almost to the point of pain as she grinds her pussy into my face. I suck at her, my fingers pistoning into her tight, slick channel in a steady rhythm.

And when she breaks, her cunt pulsing around my fingers and flooding my hand, she lets out a scream so loud, I'm sure people can hear it three buildings away.

I lick up the evidence of her release, letting her come down slowly. Only when she pushes my head away, overly sensitive, do I let her go.

My hand smells like her, musky and rich. The scent of her, combined with her subtle jasmine perfume, makes my aching cock leak behind my zipper. I adjust myself, but I don't go any further.

Pressing a soft kiss to the tip of her clit, I slide down the bed and draw the blankets around her body. Her legs spread akimbo while she drapes her arm over her eyes.

Tucking her in, I press a kiss to her forehead.

"What're you doing?" She almost sounds petulant, her words slurred.

"Putting you to bed."

Her lashes flutter as she blinks slowly. "But—you didn't come."

"This wasn't about me." *And I'm about ten seconds away from coming in my pants.* I have to pick and choose my battles.

Elsy frowns. "Wyatt…"

I shake my head. "Have a good sleep, Els. I'm leaving tomorrow night for a long road trip. Can I see you when I come back?"

"You're seeing me right now."

"And I want to see you again. When I get back."

"Okay." She yawns, her eyes heavy. "Have a good trip."

Ducking down, I kiss her forehead again.

seventeen

. . .

Elsy

HERE'S THE THING: when the guy you hate gives you a screaming orgasm and then tucks you into bed, things get confusing. When he has a week-long road trip and you can't talk it out, it gets worse.

I am entirely capable of picking up the phone and texting him. I can totally do it.

I'm just… not sure what to say.

Hey, thanks for fingering me until I nearly cried? Sorry I didn't return the favor?

He didn't *want* me to get him off. Am I that hideous that he can't stand the thought of me touching him?

No. Wyatt said over and over again how sexy he finds me. It blows my mind. I'm still trying to figure out what game he's playing. There has to be an end goal, and it's definitely not getting me into bed because he *likes* me. It's never that easy. In all those cheesy '90s rom-coms, there's always a bet for the guy to seduce the ugly duckling. But he's not *seducing* me. At least, I don't think he is.

With a groan, I rub my forehead. This is making my head hurt. The last thing I need is to fixate on this—again.

A horn honks behind me, and I startle, beeping mine, too.

I wave apologetically to the car in front of me and try to focus.

The airport arrivals area is a chaotic zoo, as it usually is. Cars are weaving in and out of the lanes, trying to pick up their passengers and leave. That's what I want, too.

At long last, I spot Bex. Getting out of the car, I rush toward her, grabbing her into a hug. I've missed my best friend.

"Girl, you look so good," she gushes. "You're, like, glowing."

"New moisturizer," I dismiss, even though all of my skincare products are exactly the same. "How was your flight?"

She groans, tossing her bag into the trunk and then climbing into the car.

"That bad?"

"Worse."

She had a work conference in Houston this week. While she was in my neck of the woods, she hopped over to Austin for the weekend. We have thirty-six hours of fun girl time before we go back to real life.

"I'm surprised Wyatt didn't insist on picking me up," Bex says carefully.

I glance over at her, surprised. "I didn't ask him."

"Are things any better between you two?"

My face warms, remembering the heat that night.

"They're fine."

"But you've been spending more time together," she says.

Shrugging my shoulders, I flick on my turn signal to merge into traffic and get out of the airport. "He's been around lately. That's all."

"Uh-huh. Sure."

Wait a second. I haven't mentioned we've been hanging out. How does she know?

"Did he say something?" I ask. "About me?"

Bex shrugs, and I have the distinct impression she's mocking me. "Not much."

Pressing my lips into a thin line, I try to focus on the road.

Her phone chimes in her hand. "I know this weekend is supposed to be girl time, but he invited us to come to practice today. Is that okay? I don't know what you have planned."

"That's fine."

I didn't know he was back. I mean, I knew the team got back into town because we have tickets to their game tonight. But I didn't know he was back and settled into his routine.

Why didn't he text me? Now that he's had his fun, is he ready to move on?

My thoughts get progressively darker as the morning goes on. *Thanks, anxiety brain.* We drop Bex's bag off at the apartment and then head out for a bottomless-mimosa brunch. The alcohol doesn't help the black cloud storming in my head.

Was all of this a game to him?

The training center is on the outskirts of downtown. It's a top-of-the-line facility with everything a hockey player could ever need or want.

The Uber drops us off at the gate, and Bex and I giggle as we show our IDs to security. They eye us suspiciously, but our names are on the list, so they let us in.

The first player we see is Riley, the rookie, wearing an Aces T-shirt and socks with slides. Wait, what is it the guys call him?

"Puppy Dog!" I call out, and Bex snickers.

His head swivels to face me, horror on his face. "No. Oh, hell no."

"What's wrong, Puppy Dog?" she chimes in.

"Fuck, there are two of you." Riley shakes his head. "Come on, let's go find Whitney."

Taking us by the hand like he doesn't trust us not to make a break for it, he leads us through the maze of the training center until we come to a lounge area with soft-looking sofas. I collapse onto the closest one, burrowing into the cushions.

"How much have you had to drink?" Riley asks. He checks his watch. "Fuck, it's not even noon."

"Boozy brunch is boozy." Bex giggles again, then hiccups. "Wyatt is going to be so upset. I can't wait."

He shakes his head. "Just—don't go anywhere, okay? Stay."

"Bark, bark," I say, before the giggles overtake me, too.

Glaring at me, he turns on his heels and stalks away. I close my eyes and sink into the pillows. They're so soft. The corduroy should be an unpleasant texture, but it's surprisingly soothing against my cheek. I could almost fall asleep right here.

"What the fuck happened?" Wyatt's voice snaps me out of my daze.

He's standing over us, his hands on his hips as he glares at us.

"Rebecca Lynn, what did you do?"

Bex burps.

He kneels in front of me, studying me carefully. "Are you okay, Elsy?"

"'M fine," I manage. "Had a few drinks. Don't be a poopy party."

"A what?" another voice says.

"Oh, great. Henry's back." My voice comes out excited, which surprises me in my brain, because that's not my usual reaction to his presence. He's *fine*, but we're not besties. "I'm still not having a threesome with you."

Muffled laughter breaks through my drunken haze.

Bex slaps her arm at me, hitting me in the boob. "You can't have a threesome with my brother. That's gross."

"I said I'm not!" I slap her back.

"Nobody is having a threesome with anyone!" Ooh, Wyatt sounds *pissed*.

Now there's laughter outright. A lot of it.

I force an eye open to find half the hockey team assembled behind him.

"It's a party!" As I push myself up to a sitting position, I'm overcome by a wave of dizziness. "I don't feel so good."

"I've got you, Els." Wyatt pulls me into his arms, half dragging me across the lounge to where a garbage can is hidden in the corner. "How much did you have to drink?"

"A lot," Bex cheers. "It was bottomless brunch."

Wyatt's hard body presses against mine. He's sweaty from his workout, but he still smells good. His citrus-and-clove soap warms me from the inside out.

"It's okay, Els." His voice is quiet, his words only for me. "I've got you."

And when the sickness overtakes me and I make use of that trash can, he holds me upright, rubbing circles on my back.

"I don't feel so good." I sag into his warm body and he draws his arms around me, almost like a hug.

"No, I don't suppose you do, sweetheart." He pushes my hair back from my face, sweaty and red from being sick. "Let me get you some water."

After leading me back to the sofa, he settles me among the pillows. Henry steps up with a water bottle and Wyatt grunts at his teammate, taking off the cap for me.

"Drink, Els. It'll help."

"I'm not a baby." Grumbling under my breath, I do as he says. The cool water feels refreshing as it slides down my raw throat. My buzz is quickly wearing off, leaving me achy and tender.

Wyatt turns to another player. I don't think I've met him yet.

"Grab Jabari," he says. "See if he can give them something for the hangover."

Beside me, Bex lets out a snore. She's passed out, her limbs akimbo.

With a sigh, Wyatt repositions his sister into an angle that's less… drunk and passed out.

"You two are trouble," he mutters.

"Ooh, you're in trouble," Henry taunts. "Spank me, Daddy."

"Fuck off," Wyatt snaps, then places the back of his hand on my forehead. "You feeling better, Els?"

I nod, but it comes out wobbly. "I think so."

But the dark is closing in on me, and it's getting harder to keep my eyes open. I blink a few times.

Wyatt leans down and kisses my forehead. I know he does. I'm not making it up.

Because the next thing I know, the darkness overtakes me.

eighteen

. . .

Wyatt

"YOU'RE FUCKED," Henry says.

"I know."

"No, I mean, you're really fucked."

"I *know*. Fuck off." I glare at him as we lace up our skates for practice.

"Does she even know you're in love with her?"

"I'm not in love with her," I say, not meeting his eyes.

Except I'm well and truly aware it's a lie.

I love Elsy Alexander. And she… tolerates me.

Henry fixes me with a look. "I don't care if you're lying to me, but at least be honest with her," he snaps. "She doesn't deserve to be jerked around."

Sagging onto the bench, I rub my hands over my face. "That's not what's happening here."

"Look, I… like her," he finally says. His voice is pained, like he doesn't want to admit it.

My eyebrows fly up. "Excuse me?"

Maybe all those jokes about threesomes are getting to him. I'm still not interested in sharing Elsy—with anyone, and especially not with a teammate. Henry might be a playboy, and there's nothing wrong with that as long as everyone is happy, but I'm not about to blur the lines.

Elsy's mine. End of story.

"I'm not trying to step in on your girl," he's quick to add. "I'm just saying, I like having her around. She's cool. If you two get together for real and have lots of little blond-haired babies, I'll be your biggest supporter."

"Let's not get ahead of ourselves."

But somehow, the thought of Elsy and me having kids isn't as terror-inducing as I expected. I've never given much thought to having kids before. I figured I'd get around to it eventually. Maybe after I retire. I'm thirty-two. Most guys my age are coasting to the end of their careers. The majority of them are already married and have families.

I'm married to hockey. That's how it's always been.

With Elsy, though… I'm starting to think I can have both her *and* hockey. Maybe. Possibly.

I want both. I don't know how I can have it, though.

She and Bex slept off their hangovers in the lounge. It's not the first time it's happened, though usually it's a player and not our friends and family. Jabari, one of the trainers, found a few blankets for them, and when they woke up, the team doctor even gave them IVs to combat the dehydration.

Puppy stood guard at the lounge door, practically baring his teeth at any players who went near the room while they were asleep. Once they were awake, giggly and happy again, he relaxed a bit.

Hey, if his career in hockey doesn't work out, he can always moonlight as a bodyguard.

I give Riley a nod as I enter the lounge after our on-ice practice and a shower. He's back at his post, guarding the two most precious people in my life.

Bex is sitting at the island barstools, eating salmon and rice. Ah, pregame fuel. Most of the other players are still in the showers or getting treatment, but in about half an hour, this place will be packed to the brim with hungry hockey players.

"Where's Elsy?"

My sister laughs. "So that's how it is."

I frown. "What?"

"Hey, little sister, how was your flight, good to see you, hope you're feeling okay," she snarks.

Rolling my eyes, I round the island and tug her into a hug.

"Rebecca Lynn. You got drunk and showed up at my work."

"Yeah, and your first question is about my best friend."

Shame-faced, I sigh. "Yeah. I guess so. Sorry."

She shakes her head, spearing a piece of salmon with her fork. "She's fine. Mitch called."

"Fucking hate that guy," I mutter.

"There's nothing going on with them," she says.

"No, I know." Elsy made it clear she's not into him that way. I've never doubted that. It doesn't take away my envy at his getting to know a part of her that I never will. He's her family. She loves him.

She tolerates me.

"Not like there is with you two," Bex says pointedly.

Groaning, I sink onto the stool opposite hers. "Shut up."

"What's going on?"

"Nothing," I mutter, grabbing her plate.

She tugs it back. "I don't believe that at all."

"I'm not talking about this with you." I run a hand over my face.

"So there *is* something going on."

I glare at her.

"Hey, I just want you to be happy," Bex says. "If my best friend does it for you, good, go after her. Don't let her get away."

"Don't intend to," I mutter under my breath.

"So what're you going to do? A grand gesture?"

"Can't I just ask her out?"

Bex pins me with a look. "No."

"Why not?"

"Because it should be… special. You've been in love with her forever."

"Shut up. It's not like that."

She laughs. "Dude, you are so far gone for her. Ever since that first night I introduced you."

And for several years before then.

Glancing around the room, I make sure we're still alone.

"So you're okay with this? We have your blessing?"

"Are you kidding?" She grins. "My brother and my best friend. What could be better? I love it."

"Don't make it weird."

"I want to be your best man at the wedding," she says. "Besides, she'll probably ask Mitch to stand up with her. I can't wait to finally meet the guy after all these years."

"You've never met Mitchell?" He's played in the league as long as I have. I'd have thought with the way she and Elsy are attached at the hip, they'd have crossed paths more than once. Then again, they'd only been living in Boston together for two years.

"Nope. Whenever he's been in town, I've had a conflict or the flu or a date. I'll meet him eventually." Bex smirks. "Hopefully, before the wedding."

"Shut up with that." I shove her off the stool and she stumbles, gasping at me.

"You asshole." She tries to shove me back, but I steal her abandoned plate and fork, taking a bite of the salmon. "Get your own food."

"But I'm hungry," I tease my little sister. She growls at me, baring her teeth.

Except she's not so little anymore. She celebrates her thirtieth birthday in a few months.

"Wow," Elsy says, walking into the lounge with her phone

in her hand. "I leave for five minutes and the Whitney siblings revert to their true forms."

I clear my throat. "How are you feeling?"

"I'm fine. That IV… no wonder you guys never have hangovers." She grins. "I could get used to that kind of recovery."

"Or you could not get drunk at brunch." I can't help the censure in my voice.

Her eyes flash. "Fuck off, Wyatt. You don't get to tell me what to do."

Irritated, I glare at her. "That's not what I'm trying to do." I only want to protect her. But I can't do that if she's getting wasted when I'm not there to look out for her.

"Really? Because it sure sounds like it."

Bex steps between us. "Okay, let's all calm down a bit here," she says, ever the peacemaker. "Elsy, Wyatt is a dick and spoke without thinking. He does it all the time."

To my surprise, Elsy's face crumples. "Yeah, I remember that all too well."

She spins on her heel, stalking out of the room. I stare after her, trying to figure out what just happened.

Bex glares at me. "Fix it," she hisses.

"How? You said it yourself, I'm a dick. I spoke without thinking."

"Go after her." She shoves me. "Show her you love her."

Fuck. That's exactly what I have to do.

Jogging after her, I track Elsy to the opposite end of the training facility where the admin offices are. I call her name and watch as a line of tension creeps into her shoulders.

"Fuck off, Wyatt," she snaps, not turning to look at me.

"Elsy," I say again.

She whirls to fight me, an argument on her lips.

"I'm sorry," I blurt. "I'm an asshole."

Surprise flashes across her face before she folds her arms over her chest. "Yeah, you are."

"The last thing I want to do is hurt your feelings."

"Well, you did." Her chin lifts in defiance. "Sorry isn't enough."

Slowly, I reach for her, and when she doesn't push me away, I pull her into my arms.

"I'm sorry for hurting your feelings. I didn't want to imply that you can't do anything you want," I tell her. "If you want to go day drinking, that's entirely your right. I would never want to take that away from you."

She melts into me, winding her arms around my neck. "Then why'd you say it?"

"Because I didn't think." I tuck a strand of her hair behind her ear and she leans into the touch. "I don't like the idea of you getting drunk and getting hurt. You can take care of yourself, I know," I'm quick to add. "But I still want to look out for you."

Her eyes are fixed on my neck. "I like that you do."

"Good. Because I want to keep doing it." My stomach twists. "Elsy, can we—can we start over?"

"Is that what you want?" She meets my eyes.

I swallow. "Yeah. That's what I want."

She pulls away. "Okay. We can do that."

Ducking my head, I aim to kiss her, but she evades my lips. And when I try to pull her back into my arms, she won't let me.

"You're going to have to work a little harder than that," Elsy says, a smirk on her lips.

nineteen

. . .

Elsy

"I SLEPT WITH WYATT," I blurt in the middle of his game. The Aces are up two scores over Vancouver, and I'm… disoriented. And for once, it has nothing to do with drinking.

Bex laughs. "I know."

I gape at her. "You—you know?"

"You haven't been very subtle," she says. "You look like you want to strip him naked. Which, gross, he's my brother."

"But—no." I shake my head. "We hooked up last week, but that's not… we slept together thirteen years ago."

Tossing some popcorn into her mouth, Bex rolls her eyes. "Yeah. I know."

"How do you know? I've never told you!"

"It's obvious he's seen you naked." She shrugs. "He always looks at you like he wants to devour you."

"No, he doesn't."

"Yeah. For as long as I've known you." Bex pauses, her eyes on the ice ahead of us. Vancouver just got a shot on goal, missing wide. "You said thirteen years ago. We've only been friends for about five. And don't get me wrong, I love you and I'm thankful for our friendship, but—"

"It was before we met." I rub at my forehead. "Then you

and I became friends, and I didn't know he was your brother until, like, a few months in when he came to visit, and then he didn't remember we hooked up, and—"

Bex's boisterous laugh cuts me off. "You think he didn't remember you?"

I pin her with a glare. "He didn't know it was me. He looked me in the eye and said nice to meet you."

"When you went to the bathroom, he told me you'd already hooked up and it hadn't gone well. I just figured he couldn't get it up and disappointed you."

Despite the chill in the air, heat floods my face, turning my cheeks pink. "That… is not what happened."

"Gross." Her nose wrinkles, but she can't hide her grin. "Well, at least he was good to you?"

I frown. "Kind of."

Her expression turns thunderous. "Do I have to beat him up?"

"No. He was—he was fine. Good, even." Hard plastic bites into my thigh as I squirm in my seat, clenching my thighs together at the memory of that night. My stomach twists as the second half of the memory comes to the forefront. "The next day, he said some things in front of his teammates, and—"

"Oh, fuck no." Bex shoves her shirtsleeves up her arms. "I'm going to punch him in the face."

I catch her arm. "Don't. It was a long time ago."

"He hurt you."

"Yeah, well…" I shrug. "I'm working on it."

Letting go of some of her hostility, she sits back in her seat. "So. You guys hooked up recently? Are you going to again?"

"I honestly don't know."

He wants to start over. All this time, I thought he didn't remember our night together. Then he opened his big, fat mouth and said something dumb—just like he had all those years ago.

Is that what he was referring to?

Rubbing at my forehead, I try to think this through.

"I'm so confused," I admit.

"I know, sweetie." She pats my knee. "We'll get to the bottom of this."

Turning to watch the game, I try to keep my attention on the ice. Wyatt plays a hard, heavy-hitting game, grinding out his minutes with Henry and Riley on his line. They're bruisers, looking to mess shit up, not so much score goals. Riley's a scrappy little dude. He's already been in a fight in his first six weeks in the league.

Henry looks like he's about a shift away from going for a tilt with the entire Vancouver defense. He's already two trips and a slash in. I'm surprised the coach hasn't benched him for forcing the team into three penalty kills in the first two periods.

Wyatt lays a heavy hit on one of the Vancouver forwards, and the ref calls him for the cross-check, even though it was a clean hit on the numbers. Scowling, he strides toward the penalty box, stewing.

He rips his helmet off and takes a drink. Our seats are behind the players' bench, so we're across the ice from the box, but I have a perfect view of his frustration thanks to the Jumbotron focusing on him. He's sweaty, his face flushed with exertion and probably irritation, glaring at the camera.

He's so fucking hot. A shiver of heat runs through me, warming me from the inside out.

"Damn," I mutter, and Bex winces.

"Gross," she says. "That's my brother you're eye-fucking."

"Yeah, well, your brother's hot." I cross my arms over my chest, like that'll hide the way my nipples have pebbled in my bra. "Besides, I just told you we hooked up."

"Doesn't mean I want to *see* it."

But she's smiling. I don't think she's nearly as put out as she's pretending.

Vancouver has the puck in the Austin zone, but no matter how many times they set up formation, they can't drive the puck home. The time on the penalty runs down, and then Wyatt is freed right as Viggy clears the puck, and he's able to pick it up on his stick. Murdock is quick behind him, and then it's a two-on-one against the lone Vancouver defenseman.

Wyatt passes to Murdock.

Murdock passes back.

And then Wyatt snipes a bullet past the Vancouver goalie.

The lamp lights up.

Three-zero, Austin.

I'm on my feet, screaming, as the bench in front of me erupts into cheers.

Murdock ducks to pick up the puck, flipping it to Wyatt. It's his first with the team. He's more of a brawler than a goal scorer, but I can't deny the happiness lighting his face. Even though he's more than a fighter, I think sometimes he gets stuck in that mentality, always on the hunt for a scrap.

I need to show Wyatt there's more to life than fighting. More to *us* than fighting.

He zooms past the bench for the post-goal celly, then takes his place on the bench. Jabari, the trainer, holds his hand out for the puck.

But Wyatt shakes his head. He makes eye contact with me and points.

"What?" I shout. "You scored. Yay."

He smirks at me, his ice-blue eyes bright. Henry turns around to see what the fuss is about and grins.

Wyatt flips the puck over the glass. Bex snatches it out of midair and he shakes his head, pointing to me.

With a knowing smile, my best friend hands over the puck, and I clutch my prize, staring at him.

"What are you doing?" I shout at him.

He grins. "Keep that safe for me, babe."

Bex elbows me. "He called you *babe*."

"Shut up." I elbow her back.

But I can't deny it feels good, like a warm glow enveloping me in a hug. I don't know what's going on between us, but there's definitely something there. Could he really have remembered all this time?

twenty

. . .

Wyatt

"DUDE, YOU'RE ON FIRE," Viggy says, clapping me on the shoulder.

"Fuck, yeah," Henry chimes in.

My natural inclination is to brush off their compliments, because I'm simply doing my job, which is ridiculous because I fucking killed it out there.

"Drinks on me," I call out to the guys. "Who's coming to O'Malley's?"

Cheers echo throughout the locker room.

"So I'm just going to ask," Puppy says. "Who's the ginger?"

I glare at him. "You keep your hands off my sister."

"Got it, got it," he says, lifting his hands in innocence. "Just asking."

"Yeah, well, you ask a lot." I glower at him.

Riley laughs. "Dude, I'm nineteen and all you posers are, like, twice my age. There aren't any chicks my age hanging around."

"Maybe because you call them *chicks*," Henry points out. "Just hit up a hookup app like everyone else."

"Don't do that," Viggy and I say in unison.

"Go to the bar, find a puck bunny, and take her home," Viggy adds. "It's not that complicated."

Riley makes a face. "That feels so… impersonal."

"Are you trying to find a girlfriend, or do you want to get laid?" I ask. "You're at the early start of your career. You don't have to settle down unless you want to. There's plenty of time to play the field."

He hums, clearly not agreeing with me.

"Look, I'm thirty-two," I point out. "I've dated throughout my career, but at the end of the day, hockey came first, and if they couldn't get on board with that, it didn't work out. Focus on yourself, on your career. Go out on the town, take a woman home, and move on. And for fuck's sake, don't get attached. Your career comes first. Always."

Henry raises his brows. "Always?"

"Until the conversation changes to forever and all that shit, yeah. Sooner than most of us would like, we have to say goodbye to hockey." I shrug. "I'm at the end of my career. I probably won't get another contract after this. I've got three more years left. Who knows what will happen?"

"And how does Elsy factor into that?" Viggy asks pointedly.

"We're not together, so right now, she doesn't," I tell him honestly. "If something were to change with us, if she wanted something serious and not casual, then it's something I'd address with her. Between the two of us, we'd figure it out."

Things have shifted so rapidly. I don't know what she wants. Hell, I don't really know what *I* want.

Other than her. I want her in my life, in my bed. The rest of it? No clue.

Guess I should probably figure that out before I ask her.

When she agreed to a do-over, it was like a weight was lifted off my shoulders. I can finally breathe again. Now's my chance to prove to her I'm different, that I've changed.

Although putting my foot in my mouth this afternoon probably didn't help…

Elsy and Bex are waiting in the friends and family hallway with the other wives and partners. When I reach them, Bex darts forward and hugs me. I can't deny it's nice to be able to do this with my sister by my side. She's always supported me unconditionally, even though our parents are less than thrilled with the way my life has turned out.

Why can't they be happy for me? My life is fucking awesome. I love hockey; I love getting to travel. I hated school. Even though Bex has enough degrees for the both of us, she's never looked down on me for my lack of education or my career choices. She's proud of me.

"Good game," my sister says in my ear. "Don't fuck this up."

"I won't," I whisper to her.

She smiles before she backhands me in the gut, a love tap for old time's sake. "Good."

I cough as she knocks the wind out of me. Even though she's been done with lacrosse for eight years, she still packs a punch. Turning my attention to Elsy, I take in the nervousness in her eyes, the worry on her face.

"Glad you could make it." Feeling like an awkward pre-teen talking to the prettiest girl in school, I try to project warmth into my voice. The last thing I want is to spook my skittish kitten.

She darts forward, wrapping her arms around me in a quick hug.

But I don't let her go, even when she tries to pull away. Breathing her in, I hold her close, memorizing the soft press of her curves against my body, the light jasmine scent of her hair.

"I'm glad you're here," I whisper in her ear.

She tenses in my arms.

"Come to the bar with us?" My hand roves over her upper back. "Please?"

"Okay," she mumbles.

She usually takes an Uber to the game and I drive her home, so she's familiar with the walk to the garage. She has one arm linked through my sister's, and they're giggling ahead of me. I'm struck by the sudden need to hold her hand. What am I, fifteen? I don't know the last time I did that with a woman.

Still, I want to hold her hand.

But when I reach for her, the back of my knuckles brushing against hers, she shifts away and sticks her hand into her sweatshirt pocket.

Shit. Did I mess this up already?

I open the back door for Bex and the front for Elsy. She slides into my car like she was meant to, like the seat was made for her.

The last time we were in here together, she let me touch her thigh. Then she took me up to her bedroom and…

Somehow, I doubt that's happening tonight.

Elsy and Bex chatter throughout the drive, and when we get to the bar, I'm not surprised to find most of my teammates have already made it. A cheer goes up when we get to our reserved section.

"Now we can party," Miller calls, making Lathan laugh.

As promised, I arrange with Tina to buy the guys a round of drinks.

We crush into the booth, and somehow, Elsy gets pressed into my side, Bex beside her. As much as I want to chat with my sister, I know they need each other, too. So I settle for curling my arm around Elsy's shoulder, smiling when she leans into me. I play with a tendril of her hair, the noise of the pub filtering around me, calming some of the post-game adrenaline coursing through my system.

"You good, man?" Henry asks as Tina sets my usual burger in front of me.

"Thanks, T."

She gives me a tired smile and moves on.

"Yeah, I'm fine," I say to my teammate. "Just been a long day."

Movement in the corner of my eye catches my attention, and I turn in time to see Elsy sneaking a fry off my plate. When I tug on a lock of her hair, she looks up at me innocently.

"Oh, did you want this?" She brings the fry to her lips, preparing to take a bite.

Instead of rising to her challenge, I push my plate to the middle between us. "Have at it, babe."

Her pretty cheeks glow pink, and I duck down and bite the end of the fry, leaving plenty for her.

"Wyatt..." Her voice comes out in a whisper, but I hear her perfectly.

"Yeah?"

"What is this?"

I look around the pub. "Do you really want to have this conversation here? Now?"

She frowns.

Tightening my arm around her, I lean down to speak directly into her ear. "We're going to talk this out. But this isn't the time or the place."

Elsy swallows, so loud I can hear it. "You keep calling me 'babe.'"

"Do you want me to stop?"

She shakes her head.

"Then get used to it." I wink at her. "Babe."

Letting out a little *eep*, she flushes a brilliant red.

"Gross," Bex interrupts. "Stop flirting where I have to see you."

"You can leave," I tell my sister, not taking my eyes off Elsy.

My girl elbows me. "She's leaving soon enough."

Relenting, I give her some more personal space. I have to remove my arm from around her in order to eat my burger, but she doesn't squirm away, so I consider that a success.

I like this, having her by my side as we hang out with my teammates. They're my family, my brothers. Some of them are married, a few have kids, but mostly, they're a bunch of dudes who hang out and drink beer after games. It's nice to have a different perspective in the mix.

When the night ends, I drive my sister back to Elsy's apartment. There was never any question that Bex would stay with her. We're close, but they're closer.

I give Bex a hug goodnight, and she gives me a knowing look as she goes inside.

Catching Elsy's hand, I pull her back. She stumbles into me, her hand landing on my chest, and I take care steadying her.

"We should talk," she says softly.

My heart thuds in my chest. "Okay."

"This is…" She blows out a breath. "I don't know."

"Do you want me to stop?"

She looks away. "Um…"

"Elsy?"

When she continues to avoid my stare, chewing on her lips, my insides freeze over. If she's not interested in this, if she's not as invested as I am, I don't want to pressure her and make her resent me.

"Got it. I'll give you some space."

"Wyatt…"

"Goodnight, Elsy." Ducking down, I press a soft kiss to her cheek. "Sleep well."

twenty-one

Elsy

WHY DOES Wyatt keep pulling this shit the night before he goes on a road trip? It's like he's confusing me on purpose, like he enjoys pulling the rug out from beneath me and then scurrying away to avoid the fallout.

Logically, I know he's at the mercy of the league's schedule. He *probably* isn't trying to do this on purpose.

Maybe.

Waking up with a Whitney sibling in bed beside me, but not the sibling I want, is a reminder of why this can't happen. I can't sacrifice my friendship with Bex.

We have time for another leisurely brunch—this time, no mimosas—before she has to leave for the airport and I have to head to rehearsal. There's a performance tonight and I'm not feeling confident with the piece. I've been practicing all week, but there's a bit of tricky fingering I haven't quite been able to nail. I know I'll get it eventually, but it's going to take some work.

Anastasia is already in her seat in the rehearsal hall, her hair done up in curlers. I love that she has no shame about being authentically herself.

It also makes me glad that my go-to performance hairstyle

is a sleek ponytail braid. Practice makes perfect, and I've been doing my hair this way for years at this point.

"You okay?" she asks as I pull my violin from the case.

"Not really," I admit.

She clucks her tongue. "I'm sorry. Want to talk about it?"

Exhaling, I release some of the tension in my shoulders. "Not right now. Still trying to wrap my head around it."

"Well, if you want to chat, you know where to find me." She gives me a tight smile.

"Thanks. I appreciate that." A glimmer of happiness bubbles within me. I made a friend—an *actual* friend. It was so much easier in kindergarten. These days, it's hard work; still, I *did* it.

On instinct, I reach for my phone. I need to tell Wyatt.

But I can't.

I don't know where we stand.

We hooked up a week and a half ago. He made me feel beautiful. *Seen.*

And then he went away for a week and didn't call me.

The first time I saw him again, I was so wasted, I could barely see straight. But he took care of me, then gave me his puck. He called me babe and cuddled me in public.

It's like he's decided that I'm into him, so of course I'd want to be in a relationship with him.

And I'm not saying that's not what I want. What I object to is that he's decided all of this *for* me. I've had enough of the patronizing infantilization. I don't need another man making decisions for me without my consent. Been there, done that, lost my job and had to flee the city because of it.

Never again. I'm not going there again.

If Wyatt had just asked me out… well, I don't know that I'd have said yes, especially not right away. But he would have had a fair better shot of getting me to go along with this newly amped-up display of affection.

He remembers. All this time, he's known we slept together

thirteen years ago. So why did he let me think he didn't remember who I was? Why did he let me hate him?

That's what's bothering me the most. He's never apologized. If he acknowledges that we've hooked up, why did it take him thirteen fucking years to apologize for being an asshole in front of all his friends?

At least she put out.

If that's what he's saying in public, I can hardly imagine what he says in the privacy of the locker room. I'm not a timid wallflower, I'm not afraid to stand up for myself, but it's a lot different when he's saying the same things every other guy I've dated has said.

I'm boring. An easy lay. A sure thing. Not memorable. Not good in bed.

As much as I don't want to believe them, the fact of the matter is, multiple men have said this to me now. Surely, if three separate guys think so, there must be a shred of truth to the matter.

We run through rehearsal, and I do my job on autopilot. Most days, I'm able to lose myself in the music, but tonight, my head is in the clouds. The performance goes off without a hitch, and even though I mess up some chords, nobody in the audience seems to notice.

The conductor does, though. Some people around me do too. And Anastasia raises her eyebrows at me during the break.

I shake my head. I'm not here, not tonight.

Heading home, I pick up cheap, greasy, drive-thru tacos and a milkshake. I'm in the mood to comfort eat my feelings.

But on my doorstep is a to-go bag from the deli. When I open it, I find a tuna salad sandwich on a croissant with a tub of potato salad.

Fuck him. Just… fuck him.

He said he'd give me space. Buying me food is not giving

me space. He can't do nice things like look out for me when I'm pissed at him. How dare he?

Pulling out my phone, I'm about to give him a piece of my mind. Instead, I find a text message that must have come in while I was driving.

I miss you, he's texted.

Fuck.

How am I supposed to respond to this?

I click on his contact on my phone, but my finger slips, and I start a video call instead.

Fuck, fuck, fuck.

The tone rings loudly in the room's emptiness. I should hang up. That's the smart thing to do, right? Pretend it was an accident?

The call connects. The screen goes black as it loads his image.

My heart rate climbs to a thousand.

And I hang up.

Exhaling slowly, I press my hand over my chest, like that will make my heart rate slow down.

The stupid phone rings.

What the hell am I supposed to do?

Swallowing my fears, I accept the call.

Wyatt's tired face fills the screen. His expression clears when we make eye contact.

"Hey, Els," he says, his voice low and gravelly. The timbre makes my stomach swoop.

"Hi."

"You called me?"

"It was an accident."

He snorts. "Yeah, okay."

"Thanks. For the food."

"Any time." His face softens. "I know you had a performance tonight. Bex says you don't eat before the show."

"I get too nervous," I admit. No matter how many times I

do it, getting up on stage and bearing my heart and soul never gets any easier.

"Me, too. Before big games," he says. "Before dates, too."

My stomach swoops. "Are—are you dating?"

His lips press into a thin line, and his eyes are sad. "Not currently."

"Oh." Why does that disappoint me?

"But I'd like to," he says.

Fuck, can I get off this roller-coaster ride? It's like every other thing he says sends me over the moon and then plunges me off a cliff.

"You should do that, then. Anyone in mind?"

A burning sensation ripples through my chest as I hold my breath. I can't believe I asked him that.

Wyatt shifts on the other end of the line, bringing the phone in closer so all I can see is his face.

"Elsy," he barks. The authority in his voice makes my pulse throb. "I'm not interested in playing games. If you have something to ask me, do it."

I swallow and take a deep breath, then exhale slowly. "Who is it you want to date?"

"You. Elsy, it's always been you." His eyes pin mine. "What do you think about that?"

"I think… you could have told me."

"Told you what?"

"That you remembered." My voice breaks. "Our night together."

He chuckles. "Els, if you think I've forgotten one second of that night in the last thirteen years…"

"But… the last few years… you let me hate you."

"*I* hated myself." The words come out so softly, I lean closer to the phone to try to hear him better. "I hate that I hurt you."

"So why did you do it? Why'd you say it?" I can't hide the hurt in my voice—or the tears in my eyes.

Damn it. It's been over a decade. I thought I'd come to terms with it.

"Because I was an insecure kid who thought it would get me in cool with the guys," Wyatt admits. "I was a fucking idiot. You should have walked right up to me and slapped me across the face."

I huff a breath of laughter, though it's not funny.

"Your friend did, by the way," he adds.

"What are you talking about?"

"Mitchell broke my nose." He's matter of fact about it, and then his face creases with hurt. "I deserved it, that and ten more. I was such a dick to you. I'm sorry, Elsy. I'm so fucking sorry."

"I wish you weren't on a road trip." I need to see him face-to-face.

"We get home tomorrow midday. Can I come see you?"

Poring over his face, I don't see any ulterior motives, only earnestness.

"I have lessons until four."

"No performance?"

I shake my head. "Not tomorrow."

"Can I take you out?" Wyatt asks. "Just us, no interfering teammates?"

"Are you asking me on a date?"

"That depends," he says, a hint of a smile on his face.

"Oh?"

"Would you say yes?"

Considering, I bite my lip. "Yeah. I think so."

"Then yes, Elsy," Wyatt says, warmth in his voice. "I'm asking."

twenty-two

. . .

Wyatt

I'VE SHOWERED, shaved, and dressed in a suit and tie. Henry tried to tell me I was going overboard by bringing two dozen roses, but when Elsy opens the door, I know it was all worth it.

A sleek, dark green dress hugs her every curve. Her hair is pulled back from her face, the blond curls fanning out over her shoulders, and her makeup makes her look like herself, only amped up to ten.

But it's the look of appreciation in her eyes that takes my breath away.

"Elsy, you—"

She shuts me up by grabbing me by the tie and yanking me closer. The flowers drop to the floor as I pull her into my arms mere seconds before her lips crash into mine.

It's like a puzzle piece inside my soul is set into place. This. This is what I was missing. This is what I've needed.

Her lips rove over mine, taking control. Her tongue licks into my mouth, tasting me, tangling with my own.

A growl rumbles through me, and I crush her to me until we're fused together and it's impossible to tell where she ends and I begin.

She pulls back, gasping for breath, her chest heaving. She looks beautifully ravaged, her lipstick mussed. I lick my lips, desperate for one more taste of her.

"I'm sorry," she blurts, as I duck down to retrieve the flowers.

"Don't be sorry. What are you even sorry for?"

"I… mauled you." Her cheeks flush a pretty pink. "I just attacked you."

"I'm giving you free permission to attack me. Any time." I thrust the flowers into her hand. "For you."

"Wyatt…"

"You look gorgeous, Elsy." My eyes rove over her body again. "I almost wish we weren't going out tonight."

Her eyes flash. "Excuse me?"

"Right now, I want to stay in and lick every fucking inch of your body." I drink her in and shake my head. "We'll just have to table that for later."

"Yeah, later," she echoes. Exhaling, she straightens her shoulders. "Let me put these in water."

She gestures me into her apartment and I take in her space. I didn't get a very good look the last time I was here. A painting of a single white daisy on a black canvas hangs on the wall above her couch, and another is mounted above the fireplace, this one a bright teal portrait of more flowers. A planter sits in the window, filled with herbs.

"So you like plants?" I ask, tucking my hands in my pockets.

She hums, arranging the flowers in a vase. "I like pretty things."

"You're a pretty thing."

Elsy rolls her eyes. "I already agreed to go out with you. You don't have to say things like that anymore."

Crossing the room and setting my hands on her hips, I cage her in from behind.

"Babe," I whisper in her ear. "You are a pretty thing."

She shivers.

"Now let me take you out and prove to you that you are the most gorgeous person in every room."

Turning in the circle of my arms, she winds hers around my neck. "You're pretty confident for a guy on thin ice."

"Good thing I skate for a living." I tease a kiss across her lips. "Let's go."

After a moment to refresh her lipstick, we head out. She lets me hold her hand on the walk through her building, then when we're in the car, she takes my hand and sets it on her thigh.

She's initiating.

Maybe I have a chance with her after all.

The upscale steakhouse is a little sultry. The low lighting sets the mood, and when we're ushered to our table in a quiet corner, Elsy's feet tangle with mine.

"This is… nice."

I raise my eyebrows. "That doesn't sound sincere."

She shrugs. "You don't have to work that hard to impress me. You have money. That doesn't do anything for me."

"Us being here has nothing to do with money," I reassure her. "I brought you here because the food is supposed to be good. Yeah, I want to impress you. I've got a lot of making up to do. And if that starts with good food, good wine, and some good orgasms for you, I'll consider that a job well done."

Her cheeks pinken, but she lifts her chin and stares me down. "Awfully bold of you to presume I'm letting you in my pants again anytime soon."

My stomach twists, but if you can't be confident, fake it until it's true.

"It doesn't have to happen tonight. I'm not in a rush."

That's not a line. As much as I'd love for us to resolve this and put everything behind us, I know getting into her heart is more important than getting into her pants.

Although if she were down for both, I wouldn't say no…

Elsy raises her eyebrows. "You're not?"

"I figure I've still got a lot to make up for. Thirteen years of it, actually."

Her brilliant blue eyes sparkle as she purses her lips. "We'll see."

I fucking love that she doesn't let me off the hook. When we met, I epically screwed up; I recognize the gravity of what I said, and I'm ready to take ownership of that, to prove that's not who I am.

The waiter takes our orders and our menus, and when I reach for her hand, I'm gratified when she lets me.

"I have a lot to make up for," I tell her softly. "If it takes me the rest of my goddamn life, I'll prove to you that I'm not that guy anymore."

She frowns. "I want to believe you. Really, I do. I just—"

"You've been hurt before," I return. "By me."

"And others." Her eyes flick away before they meet mine. "I'm not… my exes…"

My stomach twists into a tangled knot as I swallow. "Did they hurt you? Physically?"

"Just words." Her bitter smile tells me plenty, and I don't like it one bit. "But their words did enough."

"Fuck, Elsy. I—I'm so sorry. For me, for them. For all of us. You didn't deserve that. You never deserved to be treated that way."

"It's fine." Her hand twitches like it can flick the thoughts away.

But I reach out and lace our fingers together, cursing the table separating us. "It's not fine. Nobody should have to deal with that. Nobody. And you—you just take it with a smile."

"I'm not always smiling," she says, deadpan.

I fix her with a look.

She breaks, letting out a small smile. "Okay, I smile a lot. So what? It's a defense mechanism."

"I just wish you didn't have to."

She blows out a breath. "Yeah. Me, too."

The waiter delivers our wine, pouring hers full. I wait for him to leave before I lift my glass to hers.

"To new beginnings," I toast, my eyes lingering on hers.

She clinks her wineglass against mine and then takes a sip.

I barely taste the merlot. It's fine, it tastes expensive. It doesn't really do anything for me. But this is part of the deal: wine and dine, fancy dress, nice suit. As much as I don't particularly care for it, I know it's what Elsy deserves. I'd give her the moon if I could.

If she lets me in, I'm sure there will be plenty of nights where we go to the pub, drink shitty beer, and eat nachos or burgers. There could be lunches at the deli or picnics at the park.

But that's for the future. Right now, I have to pull out my A game.

She asks about my road games against Ottawa and Montreal, I ask about her performance the other night and how her lessons are going. She's found a few more students, so while they keep her busy, the extra income is helpful.

I wish I knew people who were interested in learning the violin so I could help her find more students.

When our steaks arrive, we dig in, but I notice her hesitation. She doesn't look nearly as happy as I'd have thought when I planned this evening.

"You know, we don't have to do this," she says.

I look up in surprise.

"The dinner, the wine, the flowers. All of it." She waves her hand at the room. "I'd be happy with eating takeout on the couch."

"I'm sure we'll do that, too." I take her hand. "But you deserve the best, and I don't ever want you to think I'm not treating you the way you deserve. I'd do pretty much anything for you, Els."

She frowns. "You don't call me names any more. Elsabeth, Elizabeth, Eleanor… You stopped doing it."

"You told me you didn't like it," I say simply.

"I've been saying it for years."

"No, Elsy. You said to stop. I thought it was our thing." Steadily, I meet her eyes. "As soon as you told me you didn't like it, I stopped."

"As easy as that?"

"Yeah. Just like that. You never have to be subjected to something you don't consent to. It was my understanding we were both playing a game. I didn't know you weren't participating. As soon as I found out, I stopped."

She's quiet as she sits across from me, fidgeting with her napkin.

"Tell me what you're thinking."

"I'm just… processing," she finally says. "You're not who I thought you were."

"And is that a bad thing? That I'm not that guy?"

Elsy presses her lips into a line. "I'm not sure yet. Still figuring it out."

Heart racing, I squeeze her hand. "Well, let me know when you decide. I'll be waiting for you."

twenty-three

. . .

Elsy

HE'S DOING EVERYTHING RIGHT. So why can't I get out of my head?

Wyatt takes my hand as he walks me up to my apartment. My palms are sweaty. If he notices, he doesn't show it.

Do I invite him in? I don't know if I want to sleep with him. I mean, I do, because he's fucking hot in that suit, and sue me, I'm human and horny.

But I don't know if I'm mentally ready for it. I've forgiven him—for now—but I'm still on the lookout for any other unacceptable behavior. Hypervigilance is exhausting. Will I ever be able to trust him for real?

To my surprise, Wyatt stops outside my door and kisses my cheek.

"Thank you for coming out with me tonight."

My eyebrows dart up to my hairline. "You asked me out."

He clears his throat. "I did, yeah."

"You don't have to *thank* me for that."

"Elsy, you look—incredible. And if you think for a second every fucking guy in that restaurant didn't wish you were there with them, you need to get your eyes checked. So, yes, thank you. Thank you for going out with me, and thank you for giving me a chance." Wyatt's eyes hold mine. "I'm not taking this lightly."

Exhaling slowly, I find my key and open the door. "Do you want to come in?"

A smile stretches his face from ear to ear. "There's nothing I'd like more."

"I don't know that I'm ready to have sex," I admit. "I just…"

He steps closer, his fingertips on my chin, tilting my head up. "What is it?"

"I'm not ready for the night to end."

Leaning down, he brushes a soft kiss across my lips. "It doesn't have to. Whatever you want, I'm yours."

And that's how we find ourselves, twenty minutes later, sitting on the couch with a bowl of popcorn and another bottle of wine, a cheesy Hallmark movie on the TV. I've scrubbed off all my makeup and changed into sweatpants, my hair tied back in a messy bun. When he saw the bottles and pots lining my bathroom counter, he asked what they were for, so of course I had to put a clay mask on him. I mean, he did say *whatever I want*.

"It feels weird," he says, poking at his face again.

"Don't touch it." I bat his hand away.

He pulls me into his side, his arm wrapped around my shoulders. His cologne tickles my nose in the best way, his familiar scent reassuring. He took off the tie and his shirt, leaving him in a thin cotton undershirt and his suit pants. It's a good look for him.

I'd like him better if he were shirtless, though.

But that would mean opening that box I'm not sure I'm ready for.

When the timer goes off, I drag him into the bathroom to take off the mask, then slather his face in moisturizer and apply a softening lip balm.

"Is this a hint?" he asks, inspecting the lip balm. "Should I be using this more often?"

I can't hide my smile as I reach up and press a light kiss to his lips. "Only if you want."

His hand lands on my hip, drawing me close, and he kisses me more firmly.

"Only if *you* want."

He's putting the ball in my court. I'm in control here.

Threading my fingers through his, I pull him back to the couch, then shove him onto the cushions. I slide in beside him, drawing his arm over my shoulder and setting my hand on his thigh.

Wyatt tightens his arm around me, pressing a soft kiss to my temple.

"I wouldn't have thought you'd be so physically affectionate," I say casually.

"Really? Why's that?" He traces little circles on my bare shoulder.

"Because you went out of your way to avoid me before."

He laughs. "That's because I was trying not to get a hard-on in public."

I turn to him, my eyebrows raised. "What?"

"You're fucking hot. Even when you hated me—especially when you hated me—I thought you were the most gorgeous woman I'd ever seen."

My face falls. "But you let me hate you. For *years*."

"Because I deserved it. I was such a dick." A frown pinches his face. "Elsy, I'm so, so sorry. I don't know how else to say it."

I focus on the bob of his Adam's apple. "I can't forget it. It plays on a loop in my head, over and over."

He swallows, the sound audible over the softly playing music filtering through the restaurant.

"I can't forget it," I repeat. "But I may be able to forgive you one day."

"That's all I want," he says. "If I could go back and change things…"

"But we can't." I take a sip of my wine to steady myself. "Maybe it's for the better this way."

"We wouldn't be here now," he agrees. "I was nowhere near ready for the kind of relationship I want with you now. We were nineteen. We never would have lasted." He gives a self-deprecating laugh. "Between us living on opposite sides of the country, my dropping out of school, then working my way up through the AHL and into the league… I never would have been able to give you what you deserve."

"So you don't think I'm a *tubby butterface with good tits*?"

Fuck, even saying the words drags me back into that mental headspace.

"You have great tits, but you are not a butterface. You are so fucking gorgeous."

"You didn't say anything about the tubby part." My hands shake.

"I like your body." His hand skates over my side, his fingertips brushing my rolls, and for once, I don't flinch away. "I like you exactly the way you are. I've shown you how sexy I think your body is. That hasn't changed. If anything, it's even hotter now."

"I've seen pictures of your ex-girlfriends. They were tall and skinny and—"

"And they're *ex*-girlfriends. Not current. Not future."

My mouth goes dry. "Is that what we are?"

"It's what I want." Wyatt skims his fingertip over my cheek. "I'm not interested in playing games. I want you, Elsy. I want to be with you. The only question is if you're ready to be with me."

"I—I—"

He brushes a soft kiss to my lips. "I don't need an answer right away. We can work together to get there. If you're just looking for a fling, I'll say goodnight and go home. I want something real. And I think we can have it—together."

"I'm not ready to have sex." The words fly out of my mouth, and horrified, I bring my hands to my lips like that will reverse them.

He pulls my hands away. "That's fine. Did I say I expected us to dive into bed?"

I pause. "Well, no. But guys usually—"

"I'm not them." His voice is firm and steady, a hint of steel. "I won't treat you the way they did. *I'm not them.*"

Forcing a chuckle, I try to downplay it. "So clearly I have some baggage."

"Babe, we've all got baggage. But I swear to you, we will take this at your pace. What we have, right now, it's fragile. It's so delicate. We have to take care of it." He traces his thumb over my cheek. "Because Elsy, this thing we have... it could be really, really great. I'm certain of that."

"I want it. Want that." My words come out in a whisper. "I just..."

Wyatt's eyes are kind as he peers at me. "We take this at your pace. Whatever you want."

"And if I'm never ready for sex?"

He shrugs. "Then we never have sex."

"Really? You'd stay in a relationship without getting laid?"

"Yes. Because it's not about *getting laid* for me," he states. "It's about you, and us, and what we can have together. It goes beyond it. Can sex be an important part of a relationship? Yes. As long as we're working toward a future where we trust and respect each other, I'm confident that will come with time. When you're ready, you'll let me into your heart."

Marveling at his words, I shake my head. "You sound so sure."

"Confident." He kisses me, a quick, hard kiss. "You're worth putting in the work."

Swallowing my fears, I exhale slowly. "Will you stay the night?"

"You… want me to stay?"

"Yeah. I want to fall asleep in your arms. I want—fuck, I want you to hold me and tell me it will all be okay. Right now, I think I need that."

Wyatt pulls me in, wrapping my arms around his neck and his around my waist. My face tucks perfectly onto his shoulder.

"It will all be okay."

"You don't know that."

"You're right, I don't know that." His voice is a soothing rumble. "But I believe it. And that's what means it'll come true."

We stay like that for several moments, loosely embraced, before I feel ready to pull away. Rising to my feet, I offer him my hand, and he takes it without hesitation.

"Come to bed with me, Wyatt."

In the bathroom, we brush our teeth side by side. Thank goodness I bought extra toothbrushes. He finally takes off his suit pants and his undershirt, leaving him in navy-blue boxer briefs.

Fuck, he fills them out well. His quads stretch the fabric, his slim waist and cut abs on display. And his cock…

The longer I stare at him, the more the bulge grows, and he shifts, covering his crotch with his hand.

"None of that," he says, sharp, but with a smile on his face.

"None of what?" I ask innocently.

"You look like you want to devour me." He smirks at me. "There's a time and a place, but we're going to bed. *To sleep.* Come on, let's sleep."

Pulling back the covers, I slide into my favorite side, facing him. He slips in the other end of the bed and draws me close, his arms around me.

"Hi," I whisper, unexpectedly bashful.

"Hi." His smile stretches from ear to ear. "I'm really looking forward to this."

"To sleeping in the same bed without having sex?" Each word has my skepticism rising higher.

"Yeah. Because I get to hold you." He kisses my forehead. "That's enough for me."

Rolling over, I turn out the light, then scoot back to his side. I rest my head on his chest and wrap my arm around his waist, my fingertips tracing the lines of his abs.

Wyatt catches my hand, pressing it flat against his stomach.

"Please," he says. His voice is strained, like he's in pain.

"What?"

"Please don't tease me."

"I wasn't—"

"Elsy, I'm losing grip of my control. Please don't tease me." He squeezes my hand. "I'm really, truly okay with no sex. I'm not pressuring you in the slightest. But that doesn't mean you can work me up just for fun."

Propping my head up, I look up at him. "Is that what you think I was doing?"

"It might not be what you intended, but it's what's happening." Dragging my hand down his body, he stops over his crotch.

The steely length of his erection fills my palm and, automatically, I squeeze the base of his cock. My thumb brushes over the head of his dick, and I gasp at the sticky wetness soaking his cotton briefs.

His breath hitches.

"Just being around you right now is… difficult. I need you to stop touching me. *Please.*"

I withdraw my hand. "Oh. Okay."

Wyatt draws my arm around his waist again, my hand flat against his belly. "This is fine. I like this."

Setting my hand back on his chest, I squirm closer. "I like this, too."

twenty-four

. . .

Wyatt

I'M GOING TO DIE.

If I thought Elsy teasing me last night was bad, it was nothing compared to sleeping beside her all night. Her soft body curled into mine, her jasmine perfume filling my nose… it was pure torture in the best way possible.

My alarm goes off and I silence it before it can wake her. I have an early morning treatment session on my shoulder, then a meeting with my sports psychologist, all before practice and the day's workout.

My muscles feel sore and achy, like I've already played a full three-hour game. That doesn't bode well for today. I climb into the shower, ready to wash away the feeling.

The water warms quickly and I step under the hot spray. My cock bobs against my stomach, hard and needy. That hasn't waned.

Fuck. I really don't want to walk out of here like this.

Can I really do it? Touch myself in Elsy's shower? Isn't that crossing, like, ten thousand lines?

Need thrums in my veins. I want to bury my face in her pussy again, taste her on my tongue. Maybe another morning, she'll let me wake her up that way, my mouth teasing her awake.

I honestly think I might die.

Grabbing her soap, I pour some into my hand. The sweet scent of jasmine fills the humid air, surrounding me as I take my cock in my hand.

The first pass of my fist over my length makes me groan. I almost forget to be quiet and have to bite my lip. It feels so good. I got myself off yesterday as I got ready for the date, trying to take the edge off, but it feels like it's been more than a decade since the last time.

Because with Elsy, it really has been.

The shower door swings open, and my head swivels to see Elsy naked before me. She ties her hair up into a bun and then steps inside.

"You're being loud," she says. Her palm lands on my chest as she rises onto her tiptoes to kiss me. "Good morning."

"Morning," I choke out. On instinct, I release my cock, and it bobs between us.

"Oh, look, a new toy to play with." Her hand wraps around me.

"Elsy—"

Please don't toy with me. Please don't play with me.

"I'm not ready to have sex with you." Her words are as firm as her solid stroke. "But that doesn't mean you can't come. That I can't get you off."

I open my mouth, but no words come out.

"I know what I'm capable of, and right now, it's this," she says. "I'm good with this."

Pulling her into my arms, I crash my mouth to hers. She lets out a little *oof* against my lips and I smile into the kiss.

She strokes over my length, twisting her wrist when she reaches the head of my cock, then stroking again. I cover her hand with mine, tightening her grip. Together, we draw our hands down the length of my erection, and as pleasure skates up my spine and coils in my gut, I do my best to memorize this perfect moment.

Her taste, her sounds, the press of her wet, naked body against mine… this is as close to heaven as I've ever felt.

Elsy's tight fist feels perfect around my cock, her other hand on my pec directly above my heart. Can she hear it pounding? Can she hear it calling to hers?

Breaking the kiss, I drag in a ragged breath, my chest heaving.

"Elsy, you—I—"

"Shh," she says, stroking me faster now.

My hand lifts to cup her breast. Her nipples bead into tight buds, begging to be licked and sucked. I play with one, then the other, and when she doesn't protest, I nudge her hand away and bend to take her nipple in my mouth.

She lets out a gasp. "This is supposed to be about you."

"You're giving me what I want, right?" I look up at her, a smirk on my lips, and when she nods, breathless, I lave my tongue over her nipple again. "Bringing you pleasure gives me pleasure. Let me do this."

Backing her against the shower wall, I kiss and lick and suck at her perfect body. My hands rove over her flesh, digging into her ass, caressing her belly, and then move between her legs. She's slick, and it has nothing to do with the water beating down on us.

"Can I taste you?" I ask.

She pauses.

"Only if you want to. I'm fine if—"

"Please," she whimpers. "I don't know why you inside me is such a hard line, but other stuff isn't as intense. It should all be the same. An orgasm is an orgasm. But somehow… I'm more okay with that than anything else."

Standing, I give her what I intend to be a quick kiss, but she wraps her arm around my neck and holds me close.

"Just… be gentle with me," Elsy says.

"Always," I promise. "I've got your heart in my hands. That's the most precious thing in the world."

She shakes her head, her mouth curved into a smile. "You say a lot of pretty things."

"You're a pretty thing," I tell her automatically. Because she is. Because I want her to believe it, too. I'll keep repeating it until she does.

"I can think of better uses for your mouth." She pushes on my shoulder, sending me down, and I drop to my knees. The cold, hard tile is going to kill me later. It'll all be worth it, though.

I lift her leg, propping it on the tub shelf behind me.

"Just like that," I tell her, spreading her with my fingertips. Her pretty, pink clit winks at me and I give it a soft kiss, looking up at her. "You're good?"

"So good." Her face is flushed, her chest rising and falling in rapid breaths.

Diving in, I taste her, the flavor of her bursting on my tongue making my abandoned cock throb with want. I give myself a slow stroke before focusing on her again.

I warm her up slowly, alternating long, slow sucks with teasing flicks of my tongue. Her hand falls to the back of my head, threading her fingers through my hair.

When I slip a finger inside of her, she clamps around me, so tight my cock jerks. I use my free hand to touch myself with slow, leisurely strokes to keep my libido at bay. It's not my turn. There will be plenty of time for that later.

"Wyatt..." She sighs my name, and as I add a second finger, her soft, silky walls clench around me until she relaxes and sags against the tile.

Elsy rides my fingers and my mouth, tilting her hips to take more. I increase the pressure of my tongue circling her clit, drawing the bud into my mouth and flicking it. She gasps, tightening around my fingers buried deep inside her.

"Fuck." She exhales heavily. "I could come just from that."

Hey, if there's one thing I've learned in my career as a hockey player, it's how to adapt. I take instructions well.

So I do it again, and then a third time, and when I twist my wrist and brush against the spot that makes her eyes cross, I do it again.

Elsy pulses around me, her pussy milking my fingers. She grinds into my face, taking the pleasure she needs so beautifully.

When she sags against the shower wall, I drink in the sight of her, blissed-out, her face and chest flushed. I lick her release from my fingers, desperate for one more taste.

She lets out a tired giggle. "That was… wow."

"Yeah?" My knees creak as I stand up and I waste no time pulling her into arms. She buries her face in my neck, breathing me in.

"I could get used to this," she whispers.

"Oh, you will."

She grins up at me. "You seem awfully confident."

"I am." I kiss her quickly, and when she draws me in for another, I take my time. "I'm already addicted to you."

Her fingers trail down my chest, teasing over my abs, and when I don't stop her, she wraps her hand around my cock again.

She starts to lower to her knees, but I grab her arm to keep her upright.

"Don't."

Elsy looks up at me, surprise on her face. "You don't want me to?"

"Fuck, Elsy, I'm dying to see your lips wrapped around my cock. But you'll get your hair wet." And she went to the trouble of tying it up out of her way.

Her face softens. "You really are incredible."

I shake my head. "I'm really not."

"Agree to disagree." She strokes my cock again, this time with a stronger grip, the way I showed her earlier.

"I want to touch you. Can I touch you?"

She nods.

Pulling her into my arms, I kiss her thoroughly. She strokes me from root to tip, twisting her wrist at the head, and then her other hand slips between my legs to cup my balls. They're drawn up, high and tight, and all it takes is a few more strokes before I'm teetering over the edge.

Her sweet mouth on mine, coaxing little groans from me, pushes me over. I plummet over the cliff, my cock jerking in her fist as I erupt. My release splashes up her arm and onto her belly, covering her in my mark.

When I nudge her hand away, Elsy turns to the water, wiping her hands. I pull her back against my chest, wrapping my arm around her belly as I help her clean off. My chin fits perfectly on her shoulder and I kiss her neck, drinking in her scent.

Grabbing her body wash again, I squirt some of the soap onto my hands, roving them over her body. I make sure every inch of her is clean before I let her do the same to me. I'm going to smell like her all day long and I can't fucking wait. She's branded me—heart and soul, and now body, too. I'm hers.

The water runs cool and I reach over to turn it off. Elsy steps out, wrapping herself in her towel, before grabbing a second from the linen closet. I hadn't planned that far ahead.

We dress in silence. She has rehearsal this morning and then lessons this afternoon.

"Can I see you tonight?" I ask.

Elsy laughs. "Not playing hard to get?"

"Babe, I told you, I'm not playing games." I kiss her cheek. "So, tonight?"

"Maybe." She shrugs.

"Guess I'm going to have to try harder next time," I decide.

"We'll see. If this is how we're going to start the morning, you should stay over more often," she says with a teasing smile.

Dropping a soft kiss on her lips, I promise, "Anytime."

twenty-five

Elsy

WYATT HAS SLEPT over three out of the last five nights, the only time separated because of a road trip to Detroit. The two nights he had home games, I had performances, but there's something nice about knowing he'd rather come home to me than go back to his place. He shows up with food, wearing his game-day suit, and it takes everything in me not to peel it off him the second he shows up on my doorstep.

Every night, he gets me off with his fingers or mouth before he pulls me into his arms and holds me until I fall asleep. He lets me return the favor now. Touching him or sucking him is easier for me to handle than full penetrative sex. A part of me still thinks that as soon as he gets what he wants, this will end.

I make it through lessons and rehearsal, have a late lunch with Anastasia and Katrina, and then head to the training facility. Security badges me in and I wind my way through the halls to the players' lounge. There are a few Aces staff members in the hallways, people I vaguely recognize, but none that I've spoken to before. A few Aces players are still hanging around, even though the facility is open to the visiting New Orleans Thunder.

"Nicholas David Mitchell." I stand at the entrance to the lounge, one hand on the doorframe.

My best friend looks up from his plate, his fork tumbling to the table. "Elsy!" His easygoing smile stretches from ear to ear.

"You don't write, you don't call…" I choke out a laugh as my best friend lopes across the room and pulls me into a tight hug. "I missed you, asshole."

"Missed you more," he says, squeezing me until I can barely breathe.

"That your girl, Mitchell?" One of the New Orleans players asks.

"She's better than that," he says, slinging his arm over my shoulder. "She's my best friend. Basically my sister."

"He's, like, totally obsessed with me," I joke, as a few Aces players enter the lounge. I nod to Henry and Riley. "Hey, guys."

Riley eyes me curiously.

Henry reaches out and gives my arm a squeeze, his hand landing two inches below Mitch's like he's reclaiming his territory. "Elsy," he says evenly. "Didn't expect to see you today."

"You know these clowns?" Mitch asks. "I knew you've been to a few games, but I didn't realize you were on a first-name basis." He trails off. "Please tell me you didn't…"

"Didn't what?" I smile innocently up at him, but my stomach flips and I'm fairly sure he can see the manic gleam in my eyes.

I should have told him. But how do I tell my best friend, the guy who's defended me and protected me at every turn, that I'm doing something I know he won't agree with? Especially when what we have is so new and fragile.

Mitch sighs. "You and Whitney?"

"No comment."

He shakes his head. "I thought you knew better than that."

"It's fine. I'm fine. I know what I'm doing."

I think.

"We like Elsy," Riley pipes up. "She's super cool."

"And Whit is super into her," Henry tries to reassure him. "We're looking out for her."

Mitch frowns.

"They don't need to, though. This is nothing like last time."

Henry arches an eyebrow. "There was a last time?"

"It's complicated," I mutter.

My best friend snorts. "Complicated nearly got him thrown off the World Juniors team."

"I didn't know that." My stomach sinks. "He never mentioned that."

"Well, almost," he amends. "Coach didn't want the press attention."

"Still scored more goals than you in the tournament," Wyatt says from behind me.

"That's true," Mitch agrees, a smug smirk on his face. "Who's the one leading the division in points now?"

Mitch is a ruthless goal scorer. He has over fifteen points in twenty games.

"It's early in the season," Wyatt says with an easy smile. He knocks Mitch's arm off my shoulder and pulls me into his arms, kissing me softly. "Hi."

"Hi." My voice comes out breathy. Fuck. I clear my throat. "Wasn't expecting to see you here." We have plans for later this evening—*after* I go out with Mitch.

"Had a treatment session," he answers. He kisses me again. "Missed you."

"I just saw you this morning." I laugh.

"Yeah, and that was eight hours ago."

Behind me, Mitch gags. "I get it, whatever, you're together now. Can we put a lid on the PDA?"

Wyatt gives me one last kiss. "Go, have fun. Do whatever you guys are going to do."

"Just dinner, I think."

Mitch sighs. "Fuck."

Swiveling to face him, I take in his disappointment. "What's wrong?"

"Do I really have to?" he asks.

"Have to do what?"

He grinds his teeth.

"You don't have to do anything you don't want to do," I remind him. "Consent is important in more than the bedroom."

"Whitney," Mitch says with a pained expression, "would you like to join us for dinner?"

I'm surprised when Wyatt beams at him. His clear happiness at the invitation makes me smile.

"I'd love to. I know just the place."

"Is this a family affair?" Henry asks. "Can anyone join?"

My best friend sighs. "What the fuck. Why not? Who else wants to join?"

I glance at Riley curiously, but he shakes his head. "I'm not going to touch this situation with a ten-foot pole."

"Probably a good idea," Viggy says, reaching over to shake Mitch's hand. They work out together in the offseason. "We've been taking care of her."

My best friend relaxes a little. "Good. I'm glad."

"She's family," Henry chimes in, surprisingly serious. "Family means we look out for each other. On *and off* the ice."

A wave of affection washes over me. "You're not so bad, Henry."

He winks at me. "Shh. Don't tell anyone. You might ruin my reputation."

Aaaand that's the guy I've come to know.

"Okay, Mitch and I are going to hang out now," I announce. "We can go for dinner later."

Taking him by the arm, I lead him over to the couches where Bex and I passed out a few weeks ago.

"Tell me everything that's been going on with you," I demand as we get comfortable.

"Nothing's going on," he mutters. "I'm not the one who moved halfway across the country, started a new job, and started dating a total asshole. I want to hear about you."

I make a face. "Don't be like that."

"Seriously, Els?" He shakes his head. "There are so many guys out there. Hell, he has twenty-two teammates you could have gone out with. Why'd you have to pick him?"

With a shrug, I focus on meeting his eye. "I didn't want to."

"But you did."

"It just… happened. I couldn't stop it until I was in too deep. And now I don't want to."

I *like* Wyatt. I could easily see myself falling for him.

And I'm almost certain he won't break my heart again. Almost.

"He's good for me," I tell Mitch now. "He pushes me."

His eyebrows go up. "Pushes you how?"

"To go outside my comfort zone, to try new things." Glancing around the lounge, I make sure none of the players are paying attention to us before lowering my voice. "He talked me through a panic attack. He talks with me. I feel like I really know him."

"But do you?"

"I think so, yeah."

He's told me things, stuff I don't think even Bex knows about her brother. His frustration with their family is only the tip of the iceberg. He's talked about his anxiety, about the ways his therapist and sports psychologist have helped him.

What we haven't talked about is what he wants after

hockey. Does he expect a nice little wife and a bunch of kids running around? Does he want to coach or go into broadcasting?

I have no intention of giving up music. It's my career. I've worked hard to get here, and I plan to keep playing for as long as I can. Eventually, I might go back and get my PhD. Given how he feels about his family's education, will that be a deal breaker? I'm not asking him to go back to school. I respect his decision that it's not a priority for him. But that doesn't mean he'd be comfortable with me going for a doctorate.

And at the end of the day, my education is *mine*. It's my decision. I can't let him influence that. I don't think he'd tell me not to do it, but if he's uncomfortable or feeling emasculated by my career path, that's not good, either.

I really hope I have a future that includes him. Whatever that looks like... I want him by my side. I want him to support me as I reach for my goals, just as I would do the same for him.

If he can't do that, if he *won't* do that... I guess it's better if I find out now. Before I get invested. Before I get attached.

Because I'm a little afraid I'm already too late.

twenty-six

. . .

Wyatt

AFTER A SESSION with the physical therapist to work on my shoulder, a whistle on my lips, I stop in my tracks. Mitchell waits in the hallway, murderous intent on his face as he stalks toward me.

"I'm going to fucking kill you," he growls.

"Hey, there's no need for violence," I joke.

His eyes flash. "I told you *one thing*. Stay away from her. And then you—"

"It's not your place to keep me away from her." I stand my ground, meeting his eye squarely. "What she and I have is none of your business."

A promise I made over a decade ago, when I was in the lows after hurting her and his breaking my nose, hardly has any bearing on what's going on now. I stayed away from her as long as I could stand it.

Now, we're together. He can either deal with it or fuck off.

Crossing his arms over his chest, he glares at me. "You're playing with her. Leading her on."

"Except I'm not. I've been clear about my intentions from the get-go."

"This is a bad idea."

"I love her," I tell him honestly.

Mitchell gapes at me.

The words punch me in the face, and it takes everything in me not to gasp. I always thought I'd be telling her first, in some big romantic gesture with flowers and chocolate and tuna salad croissants. Not… like this. Yet the words spill from my lips, and I can't stop them. It's like once I've opened the lid, there's no putting it back inside.

"I'm in love with her. I'll do anything for her. If *she* wants to end it, I'll walk away. But you don't have the right to tell me to stay away." I square my shoulders and stare him down. "This thing between us, it's real."

I don't know when I realized it. Only that one morning I woke up in her bed and knew I wanted to do it every single morning for the rest of my life. I know that after a long, grueling game, she's the only person I want to see. And when I'm away on a road trip, all I want is to be home with her.

"I love her," I repeat. "I'm in this. I'm doing this the right way."

He grunts. "I still don't like you."

"I don't expect you to. But I hope, for her sake, we can be civil."

Mitchell evaluates me. "You're really not going away?"

"Not anytime soon."

He sighs, then extends his hand.

Taking it, we shake, and then I grin.

"You're stuck with me now."

"Yeah, yeah." He rolls his eyes. "Still think you're an asshole."

My smirk isn't intended to be taunting, but I'm fairly certain it comes off that way. "Oh, I totally am. And if you think I'm taking it easy on you tomorrow on the ice…"

"Wouldn't expect anything less."

And when we meet up at the restaurant a few hours later, Elsy by my side, I'm surprised when, after he hugs her, Mitchell offers me his hand.

"Whitney," he says evenly.

"Good to see you again," I tell him, because it's actually not a lie.

Henry approaches us, a simple grin on his face. "Elsy," he says, embracing her like he hasn't seen her in years. "You look fabulous."

"Thanks," she says, her eyes bright with happiness. She takes my hand and I squeeze hers in reassurance. "You know Nick Mitchell, right?"

"Right. We've met." Henry sticks his hand out and Mitchell shakes it. "Nice to see you off the ice, man."

The host shows us to our table. It's in an out of the way corner where we won't be disturbed. Most of the time, I don't have too many problems with people recognizing me, but after a few scary incidents back in Philly, I can never be too careful.

And considering three of us are hockey players… we attract a lot of attention.

"It's weird that I'm crashing your party. It's weird, right?" Henry asks, surprisingly self-aware. "I thought there'd be more people here. I wasn't expecting… this." He waves a hand at the intimate setting.

"Nah. You're like my annoying little brother," Elsy says, winking at him. "I know I give you a hard time, but—"

"I like it," he says quietly. Almost… shy? "I don't have any sisters. I mean, Audrey's dating Seb, but I don't get to see her every day. None of my other brothers have steady girl-friends."

She reaches across the table, taking his hand. A growl rumbles through me, but she just pats my chest and smiles at me before meeting his eyes.

"I'd love to be your sister."

Settling back in my seat, my hand on her leg, I look up to meet Mitchell's gaze. He nods at me, approval in his eyes.

Elsy asks after his dad, and as Mitchell talks, the tension in my shoulders relaxes. I've never doubted her; she says it's not romantic between them, that they've never gone there, and I believe her. It didn't keep something from gnawing at me about their friendship. I don't have any female friends. Sure, I'm friends with the girls my buddies date, but I've never had a genuine friendship with a woman I didn't want to get into bed with. I never thought that was a bad thing. Now I'm wondering how much I've missed out on.

Henry's made it clear he respects our relationship. Once I shut down the sharing idea—which I don't think he was really all that interested in to begin with—he's been exactly the same person with her. A little flirty, but not inappropriate. And it's clear now that she likes him, at least enough to want to be his pretend sibling.

Speaking of siblings, I owe Bex a call. I haven't checked in on her in nearly a week. Even though she's a grown woman and can take care of herself, a part of me feels responsible for her. She's my baby sister. If I don't look out for her, who will?

Conversation flows easily throughout dinner. Most of it is Elsy and Mitchell, but when I contribute, it feels natural. Like they want me there; like he respects my place in her life.

It must be tough, living in different cities. All of my friends are from the hockey world or tangentially related to it, so I'm used to the distance separating us because there's never been any other option. Guys get traded or sign with new teams. I don't have a lot of friends from high school, and the ones I kept in touch with, I don't see more than once a year, if that. My summer breaks are mostly spent working out by myself or with any of the guys hanging around.

I spent nine years with Philadelphia. I had a house there; I lived there year-round. My parents wouldn't let me pay off their house when I signed my first big contract, and they both still work, so I don't see the need to spend more than a week or two with them. When Bex could get away from school, I'd take her on a trip somewhere to hang out. Now that she's finished her doctoral program and isn't writing her dissertation, she has a little more flexibility, but she still only gets two weeks of vacation time a year, so she's careful about how she takes the time off.

Mostly, I spend a lot of time on my own. I've never thought there was anything wrong with that.

Until now. Until Elsy.

She lights a fire in me. She's the one I want to spend my time with. When we're apart, I'm already cataloging all the ways we can be reunited again.

And not in a creepy stalker, *I'm obsessed with you* way. More like... I finally realize what it means to want to be with another person and just breathe them in. Her presence soothes me. It doesn't matter if we're in two separate rooms, or if we're sitting on the couch and she's reading a book, or if we're curled up together talking. I feel a calmness in my soul from being around her.

I love her.

And it absolutely fucking terrifies me.

What if she's not there yet? What if she never gets there? She may have forgiven me for being a complete and utter asshole, but I know I still have a way to go to earn her heart. What if she decides I'm not worth it? My own parents don't think I'm worth anything. What if she agrees with them?

Burning pain ripples through my chest as my breathing turns quick and choppy. No matter how hard I try, I can't get a full, deep breath in. Sweat dots my hairline, and black dots dance in my periphery as my heart races. My food tastes chalky, and I have to work to swallow.

Elsy sets her hand on my arm. "Are you okay?"

I shake my head, then nod. "I'm fine," I tell her.

Her eyes narrow with concern as she studies me.

"I'm fine," I repeat, because what I want to ask instead is *what makes me so unlovable,* and that's not a question I want the answer to.

I mean, I do. But not really. I'm not ready to *hear* it. To have confirmation of all the ways I'm a failure and a fuckup. That she's only biding her time until she finds someone better and moves on.

Fuck. I rub at my chest, at the sharp, stinging sensation deep behind my pecs. It's inside of me, not surface level. The discomfort is wedged in deep.

"Wyatt, you don't look so good," she whispers. "Do you want some water?"

Grabbing blindly for the glass, I succeed only in knocking it over. The water spills onto my plate, flooding the table.

"Fuck." I dot at the mess with my napkin, but the water is spreading like a tidal wave, dumping directly onto my lap. I let out a yelp at the ice-cold rush directly over my junk.

Elsy says my name again, but it sounds far away, like she's speaking through a megaphone. No, her voice isn't amplified. A funnel? What's that word called?

A tunnel! It's like she's standing at one end of a tunnel, and there's darkness all around, and a spotlight is shining directly on me, blinding me. My ears feel plugged up, like I'm on an airplane, and my stomach swoops from the turbulence.

"Wyatt," Elsy says firmly. My eyes snap to hers, but I can't focus on her face. My gaze slips off, darting around the room. What the hell is happening?

I'm having a panic attack.

It's been a long time since the last time it's happened. They're usually isolated to hockey and I have tricks to calm down. Somehow, I don't think smelling salts will help this one. I try to focus on my breathing, on my heart beating in my chest, on the physical sensations like my clothes touching my skin or the sounds I hear.

But when I try to breathe, my throat feels like it's being

constricted. Oh, wait, that's my tie. I pull at the knot, loosening it, but it still doesn't help that panicky feeling spreading through my veins.

Elsy sets her hand on my cheek. "Wyatt," she says, more softly now. "You're okay."

Grabbing her wrist, I hold on for dear life, focusing on the simple contact.

"I'm okay." My words come out in a ragged breath.

"You're going to be okay," she repeats. "Say it."

"I'm going to be okay." My voice sounds hollow, almost far away.

"Breathe," she coos. "Take one breath in."

I do as she says, holding it, then exhaling slowly.

"Good. Again."

Following her instructions, I keep hold of her wrist, my fingers over her pulse point. It flutters beneath my fingertips, her heartbeat steady and even, and that helps me to concentrate on my breathing.

Slowly, surely, I come back to myself. The shocking cold over my lap punches me in the nuts, making my balls shrivel up all over again.

"How are you doing?" Elsy asks, her tone soothing me even more. I don't see any shame or disappointment in her eyes, only pure concern. "That looked like a bad one."

"It wasn't fun." I gulp in air. "I'm sorry. I—"

She shakes her head. "There's nothing to be sorry for. You did nothing wrong."

I frown. "But—"

She strokes her thumb over my cheek. "It happens. You can't control it."

Awareness crashes into me. Shame creeps over me as I realize Mitchell and Henry have witnessed my epic meltdown.

But there's no judgment on either of their faces.

"You good, man?" my teammate asks.

"I'm fine."

"Okay," Henry says agreeably. "But if you're ever not fine, that's okay, too. You know?"

A lump lodges in my throat, and swallowing does nothing to clear it. "Yeah. I know."

Mitchell meets my eyes steadily. "You'll be okay."

twenty-seven

. . .

Elsy

AFTER WYATT'S PANIC ATTACK, I wasn't sure what to expect. Would he draw into himself, hiding away in shame? Would he try to fuck out the lingering adrenaline?

Instead, he seems content to hold me. He's not distant, just quiet. For the first time since we started sharing a bed, he hasn't made any attempt to get me naked. We lie in the bed with his arm around me, my head on his chest, and he plays idly with my ponytail. It's nice, but I wish I could find a way to comfort him the way he's done for me. Hopefully, he'll be able to tell me what triggered him.

When I wake up, he's gone, the bed beside me cool. A note sits on the kitchen counter—*went for a run*. At least he's coming back. Guess he's retreating, then.

After a quick shower, I'm pulling out ingredients for breakfast when the front door opens. Wyatt is sweaty, shirtless, and disheveled, a takeout bag in his hand.

"Morning," he says, his voice a little less exuberant than usual as he kisses my cheek. "Sleep well?"

Okay. So we're ignoring it.

"Yeah. You?"

He sighs. "Not great."

"Do you want to talk about it?"

"I had some thoughts." He waves a hand in the air. "I still need to stew on it a little, but once I'm ready, we'll talk it out. Does that work?"

Slowly, I nod. "I just want to make sure you're okay."

"It came out of nowhere. It's usually isolated to hockey." Sighing, he runs a hand through his sweaty hair. "I booked an appointment with my therapist, and I'll probably have to start carrying my rescue meds with me. It…" He swallows, his eyes meeting mine, the stormy blue conflicted. "It scared me. To lose control like that."

I wrap my arms around his waist. My heart clenches in my chest and tears sting in my eyes. I wish I could take away his pain, but it doesn't work that way.

"I'm all sweaty," he says, keeping me at a distance.

"I don't care." Pulling him close, I tighten my grip. "I'm here for you. Whatever you need. I'm glad you're reaching out to your support network."

He rubs at his chest, like that will make the pain go away. "I don't like feeling this way."

"I don't blame you. It's not a good feeling. I've been where you are, and you've helped me through it. I want to do the same for you."

"You are." He presses a soft kiss to my lips. "You really are, and I appreciate you. So much. I don't have the words."

I rest my cheek on his sweaty chest, the hair there tickling my skin. The steady *thump, thump* of his heartbeat soothes my concern. He's not anxious right now. He's capable of rational thought.

And when he wasn't, he sought me out. He tried to handle it on his own, realized he needed help, and did what he needed to do. On top of that, he's already reached out for additional support.

"I'm so proud of you," I murmur into his chest, tears stinging my eyes. "You experienced something scary and you're not letting it drag you down, you're taking care of yourself."

He makes a noise of assent. "It's hard. I couldn't do it without you."

"Yes, you can." Looking up at him, I wait until he meets my eyes, holding his gaze. "You can. You are entirely capable of taking care of yourself. You've done it before, and you'll do it again. It's hard to recognize that inner strength, but you are strong and capable. I believe in you."

He swallows loudly. "Thank you."

"For what?"

"For believing in me. For encouraging me." He cups my cheek. "I lo—"

Wyatt stops, cutting himself off.

"What?"

He shakes his head. "I really value you," he finally says. "I'm very glad you're in my life."

"Wouldn't have it any other way."

***

The arena is already packed by the time I get there. The players are still on the ice for warm-up, so as I hurry to what's become my seat behind the bench, I try to swallow my nerves. I've been wearing a generic Austin Aces sweatshirt for each game, but I always, *always* wear Mitch's jersey. First with Seattle, then Calgary, and now in New Orleans, he sends me a jersey and I wear it the one or two times a year I get to see him.

But I've never been dating a player on the opposing team before.

Wyatt hasn't offered to give me his jersey. If it were any other guy, I'd wonder if there were doubts as to our relationship, but the way he interacts with me around his teammates, not hiding or ashamed of me, I think he's waiting for me to make the first move. He's giving me space to decide if I'm in this, like he promised, but I think it's pretty well established that we're together by now.

Next game. Once Mitch is gone and I don't have to split my allegiance, I'll ask Wyatt for a jersey. I want to proclaim to the world that I'm his.

Tonight, though, I want them both to win. Technically, that can't happen; one team will walk away the victor. As much as I want Mitch to do well, I want Wyatt to win. All the time. Every game. I'll gladly comfort him after a loss and I'll cheer with him for each win, but I'd rather there be more good times than bad.

On the ice, the players are skating in circles to get their legs going, stick handling or trying to shoot on Rempel. The guy in the navy-and-gold Whitney jersey—my guy—has his back to me as he stretches and warms up his hips. I feel no guilt whatsoever as I check him out, his ass on display as he flexes his adductor. Fuck, I wonder what it will be like when he finally fucks me, my fingers digging into his rock-hard ass as he pounds into me.

Heat flares through me, and I fan my face. I can't help it; my boyfriend is fucking hot. We're still fooling around, but I think—I think I'm ready. He stood his ground with Mitch, putting our relationship first. If I can't trust him after that, I don't think I ever will.

I want to trust him. I *need* to trust him. Otherwise, what are we doing? Why should I keep dating someone I can't rely on not to break my heart?

Wyatt gets to his feet, skating in a circle around his half of the rink. His eyes rove over the crowd, taking it all in. I do the same before every performance, that little *holy fuck, this is really happening* surprising me every single time.

Our eyes lock, and I grin at him, waving happily.

Wyatt stops in his tracks, another player nearly slamming into him.

Oh, no. Is something wrong? He's motionless, his face hard.

Should I not be here?

A murderous look crosses over his face before he skates to the gate door.

"What are you wearing?" he yells.

People are staring now, trying to figure out who he's talking to, but there's no doubt in my mind this is between us. Because of me.

My stomach sinks. I turn my back, showing the Mitchell nameplate on my back.

"Take it off," he shouts, his face red.

I open my mouth.

"Take his fucking name off your back," Wyatt yells.

Before I can blink, he's stripping off his own jersey and balling it up into his fist.

A stilted cheer ripples through the crowd. He doesn't wear a guard under his shirt, just his pads, and his muscular chest and abs are on display for fifty thousand people as my boyfriend glares at me.

My hands shake as I pull off Mitch's jersey. I'm wearing a long-sleeved shirt underneath as I crumple the New Orleans jersey into my bag.

Hands on my hips, I glare at Wyatt. "Happy now?" I demand.

He leans over the gate, tossing his jersey over the glass. I snatch it out of the air before anyone else can get to it.

"Put it on, Elsy," he shouts. "Show everyone who you belong to."

Fuck. Everything in me liquefies as I pull on his sweaty jersey. Bringing the collar to my nose, I inhale his scent, his soap and sweat and musk combining to make me throb.

"You're mine," he growls, his eyes locked on mine. "Not his."

I shake my head. "Not his. Only yours."

He looks me over, a satisfied smirk on his lips. "Don't forget that."

I won't. Not anytime soon.

Jabari, the trainer, thrusts a new jersey into Wyatt's arms. I can't hear what he says, but it's probably something like *get dressed and stop making an ass out of yourself*, because Wyatt pulls it over his head.

His teammates are laughing, and I spot Henry waving up at me, a smirk on his face. Mitch is on the other side of the ice, shaking his head and smiling. The crowd doesn't know how to react.

And fuck, neither do I. I didn't think I'd like the caveman possessive thing, but I can't deny it was hot as fuck.

Now I have to figure out a way to recreate that in the bedroom. If my boyfriend doesn't fuck me soon, I'm going to spontaneously combust.

twenty-eight

. . .

Wyatt

"YOU'RE SUCH AN ASSHOLE," Mitchell says to me as we find our seats at the pub. Henry and Puppy are beside him, arguing over who played the better game tonight.

It was me. I played the best game of my life. I didn't score any goals, but I laid some fantastic hits—including on this schmuck.

"Not denying it." I can't help my smug smile as I help Elsy into her chair, then take my own beside her, my arm draped around her shoulders.

"You just had to make a scene," he continues, shaking his head mockingly. "Such an attention whore."

"Hey, it worked. She won't be wearing your name again."

Elsy rolls her eyes. "Yes, yes, I'm yours and now everyone knows it. Thanks for that."

I squeeze her arm. "Well, I didn't think yelling out I love you in front of fifty thousand people was very romantic."

Her jaw drops.

"Fuck." I wasn't supposed to say that. I definitely wasn't supposed to blurt it out with absolutely no finesse.

"You lo-love me?" Her eyes go wide and glassy, like she's trying not to cry.

Mitchell laughs. Loudly.

Fucker. I want to flip him off. It takes everything in me not to.

Turning to her, I take her hands in mine, my eyes locked on hers.

"I probably should have said that better," I admit.

"Say it again," she demands. "I need to hear it. For real."

"I love you, Elsy." My heart thuds in my chest, trying to merge itself with hers. "I'm so fucking in love with you. You're the light in my life."

"Is this because of last night?"

"Even before the panic attack. I've been trying to find a way to say it for a while now, I just didn't have the words. Even now, I'm not sure I do. I just—I love you so fucking much."

She makes everything better. Every second I'm away on a road trip, I'm counting down until I see her again. When we're apart, my only desire is getting back to her. She settles my system in a way nothing else ever has. I'm not crawling out of my skin with anxiety. Yes, it's still there, but it's tamed, beneath the surface. It'll never go away, not completely, but I can live with it.

When I go to sleep at night, she's my last waking thought, and when I wake up, she's the first thing I want to see. Her happiness supersedes mine. Her wants and needs are my priority.

Above it all, it's the way I know she prioritizes my wants and needs, too. There's a careful balance to it, but it's a tentatively stable ebb and flow. We take care of each other. We prioritize each other.

It took us a while to find our way here, but now that I know what true happiness is, I never want to let her go. Not again.

She sniffles, her eyes glassy.

"I'm saying this all wrong. I'm sorry. Pretend I didn't say it. I don't want to ruin what we have."

Elsy wipes at her eyes. "You said it. You didn't ruin anything."

"But you're crying."

"It's not ruined," she insists. "It's better now."

"So…" I wait expectantly for her to say it back.

She lifts her eyebrows, a teasing smile on her face. "So?"

She knows exactly what she's doing and I love her for it.

"Do you love me?" I hold my breath. What if she's not there yet? What if she doesn't feel the same?

There's no need to rush. We don't have to be in the same place as long as we're on the path together.

"Eh." She shrugs, her eyes bright with mischief.

I stare at her. "Eh?"

"Eh. I'm getting there." Her hand lands on my cheek, her calming touch so familiar. "I like you a lot. I'm crazy about you. But love? Eh."

Laughing, I kiss her, and she kisses me back, and we're finally, finally one. She winds her arms around my neck, smiling against my lips.

"I'm fucking crazy about you, Wyatt Whitney," she whispers. "You make me so incredibly happy. Every day."

"That's all I want. You and me, happy." I breathe her in, her subtle jasmine perfume heating my bloodstream. "Can I take you home?"

She nods insistently. "Yes. Please."

A throat clears, and I realize Mitchell and Henry are watching us—along with half of the team.

"After we spend time with your bestie," I add belatedly.

Elsy laughs. "Yeah, okay. That can work."

"You're adorable," Mitchell says, a teasing smile on his face. He lifts his beer in toast. "I'm happy for you, Els."

"Thanks. I'm happy for me, too." She winks at me and my smile stretches my face as she curls into my side.

Tina delivers our burgers. After the last few weeks, we don't even need to order anymore. She's brought Elsy's with no tomato products, whereas mine is slathered in ketchup.

We eat and drink and talk and laugh. Mitchell is a lot more chill now that he can see firsthand how we are together.

A younger, more insecure version of me would have been ashamed of him witnessing my panic attack. A part of me might have been afraid he'd mock me for it, or spread it around the league that I'm a weak crybaby who crumbles under the pressure.

I'm not weak. I'm not a crybaby. And I might splinter sometimes, but I don't crack under the pressure of playing in the most elite hockey league in the world. If anything, I thrive under the gun.

I've come a long way from the scared, insecure person I was the last time we were playing together. I'm not that same guy anymore. Finally, I think I've proved that to him.

I'll treat Elsy like the queen she is. I'll take care of her in every way she'll let me. And most importantly, I'll be there for her, through thick and thin, no matter where her career—or mine—takes us.

It's too early to talk about marriage. Hell, I don't even know what I want to do after hockey, whenever that will be. There's too much up in the air.

But there's one thing I know for certain: Elsy is the one for me. I can bide my time until she gets on my level. I'm not going anywhere—not without her.

———

After giving Mitchell a long hug goodbye, Elsy slips her hand into mine.

"Let's go home," she says. She sweeps her gaze over my body, everything inside me heating.

As soon as I help her into the car and slide in beside her, her hand lands on my thigh like it belongs there.

Before I shift the car into gear, I lean over and kiss her, my hand diving into her hair.

"I love you," I murmur against her lips. She smiles into the kiss, fisting my tie to bring me closer.

"Take me home," she repeats. "I need you."

My heart hammers in my chest cavity, trying to break free.

"Anything you want." My voice is hoarse and raspy.

Elsy gives me a teasing smile, her hand sliding up my thigh, dangerously close to my hard-on, until I move her palm back to my knee. As much as I crave her touch, I know if I let her play, we'll never stop. And I don't really want to fool around in the car. The SUV's back seat is way too small for someone of my size and the things I want to do to her.

Instead of heading to her apartment, I drive to my condo. I live only a few blocks from her, but I've always gone to her place; I've never brought her to mine. In the last few weeks, I've barely spent any time here, only coming home for pregame naps and to pack for road trips.

"Where are we going?" she asks when I pass her street.

"Do you trust me?"

She nods readily. "I don't like surprises."

When we hit a red light, I look over at her, her blond hair shining in the moonlight. Her dark eyes are focused on the road ahead.

"We're almost there. Can you trust me for a few more minutes?"

Although she fidgets in her seat, Elsy nods again. "It'll be worth it?"

"I hope so."

I wasn't hiding my place from her, but I know she thrives with a routine and likes her creature comforts. There wasn't a reason I kept her from coming over; it was simply easier to go to her. I didn't want to make things any more complicated or give her any more reasons to end this.

But now… I'm ready to fully incorporate her into my life. No more holding back. No more half measures.

As I pull into my building's garage, the gate lifts automatically, and she looks at me with surprise.

"Is this your place?"

Nodding, I navigate to my parking space, throwing the car into park. As I round the hood, I run my sweaty palms on my suit pants, then open her door.

She takes my hand, as natural as breathing, and I lead her to the elevator.

"I know we have different jobs, and our incomes aren't the same," I start as I hit the button for the penthouse. "When you're ready, and I'm absolutely not rushing you, I'd love for you to live here. With me."

Elsy gapes at me. "You want me to move in?"

"When you're ready. I know you just moved into your apartment, so you probably have a lease. And we're so new." I squeeze her hand. "But that's my goal. I'm okay if it doesn't happen anytime soon."

She cocks her head. "Wait. So you *don't* want me to move in?"

"I want us to figure out a timeline that works for us, that doesn't adhere to any arbitrary schedule."

We reach the fifteenth floor, and I swipe my fob at the door.

"I just want to be with you. However you'll let me."

twenty-nine

. . .

Elsy

WYATT'S CONDO is fucking gorgeous. He flips a switch, and warm, bright lights bathe the room. Everything is sleek chrome and marble with top-of-the-line finishes. The kitchen is beautiful, all black cabinets with a professional-grade range.

Dumbstruck, I follow him into the main living area. Floor-to-ceiling windows look out onto the Austin cityscape. A leather sectional sits in front of a massive TV and what looks like every gaming console known to man.

He sticks his hands in his pockets, nerves clear on his face. "So? What do you think?"

"Why are you slumming it in my tiny little apartment every night when you could be here?" I can't stop staring.

He pulls me into him. "Because you're there. I want to be wherever you are."

Melting, I sway into him. He's strong and steady, the familiar scent of his cologne doing funny things to my heart rate.

"Take me to your bed." Winding my arms around his waist, I gaze up at him. "Show me how you love me."

Before I can so much as blink, he scoops me up and tosses me over his shoulder.

"Wyatt! You're going to hurt yourself." I try to wiggle free, but he sets his hand on my back, holding me steady.

"I've got you," he says, his voice calm. "I won't let you fall."

He walks me through the apartment, kicking open a door. Then deposits me in a giant bed, nestling me among the world's softest pillows.

At the foot of the bed, Wyatt strips off his suit jacket, then rolls his shirtsleeves up his forearms. I shiver, greedily drinking him in.

"You like this?" He taunts me by flexing, the veins in his forearms standing in stark relief.

And that's not the only thing standing. His pants are tented over the thick length of his erection, drawing my attention. My mouth waters, remembering his addictive, salty taste, how powerful I feel when I bring him to his knees.

Can I do this? Am I ready for this?

He distracts me by reaching for me, pulling me toward the edge of the bed. He takes off my sneakers and socks, then runs his thumb up the arch of my tender foot. I wear heels when I have to for work, but most of the time, I'd rather be in my Keds.

Impatiently, I shove my leggings off my hips, and he helps pull my legs free from the stretchy fabric. I move to take off the jersey—his jersey—but his hand lands on mine.

"Leave it," he says roughly.

He teased me earlier; it's only fair I return the favor.

My eyebrows lift as I raise the hem a few inches. "Or what?"

Wyatt lets out a growl. "Don't play with me, Elsy."

"Should I change into another one? I have so many, you know."

Before I can so much as blink, he grabs me by the hips,

yanking me down the bed. He manhandles me onto my belly, then pulls down my panties and buries his head between my legs.

He's not gentle or sweet. No, he dives in like he's starved, eating me out with a vengeance. A hand slips around to rub at my clit, hard and demanding. The scrape of his stubble between my thighs sends me climbing higher and higher. My hips lift, desperate for more as I grind against his fingers.

He grabs my ass, stroking the flesh there before he smacks me, the sharp crack echoing in the room, punctuated by my pants and moans. Need grips me by the throat as I squirm, wanting more. He spanks me again, the sting blooming into pleasure as he licks through my slick folds.

But it's not enough.

"Fuck me." My words come out on a pant.

He stills behind me. "Elsy…"

"Wyatt, I need you. Fuck me."

"Are you sure?" He pulls back, running a finger over my entrance, stopping short of pushing in. "We don't have to."

Over my shoulder, I glare at him. "If you aren't inside me in the next five seconds…"

He swallows, hurrying to his nightstand, and pulling out a condom and a bottle of lube. His clothes go flying before he suits up and slicks his fingers with the lube.

We've already had the talk about condoms; he's allergic to latex, so he uses polyurethane, which means extra lube. Both of our test results came back negative, but since I'm not on birth control, condoms are required. And frankly, even if I were on birth control, I'd probably still insist on them. It's not a trust thing; it's an anxiety brain thing. I know I'd be obsessing over getting my period every month, poised to freak out at any slight deviation in my cycle. The last thing I want is a pregnancy scare in a brand-new relationship.

Wyatt maneuvers behind me, his hands on my hips. He

presses a kiss on the back of my shoulder. "You feeling good?"

"I'll feel better once you fuck me," I snap, twitching my ass back.

The head of his cock notches against my entrance and I press against his thick length. He lets me take the lead, lets me use him like my own personal toy, until my ass rests against his thighs.

His thick length stretches me to my breaking point. The sensation of fullness is nearly overwhelming. Draping his body over mine, he rests his hands on either side of mine, his thighs bracketing my legs. He cages me in, enveloping me in his embrace.

"Fuck, Els." His shuddery breath in my ear sends a shiver down my spine. "You feel so good."

I have no words. I clench around him, his cock buried deep inside of me, and his rattling groan reverberates through his chest and into me.

Turning my head, I meet his lips in a heated kiss. He licks into my mouth, his tongue plunging in. He tastes like me, and I let out a soft whimper that has him smiling into the kiss.

"I fucking love you," he whispers.

Lifting off his cock, I drive my hips back to take him inside me again. "You mean you love fucking me."

"That, too." He gives me another kiss before he lifts himself off me, his hands moving to my hips for balance.

"Then get to it."

He laughs! He actually fucking laughs while he's buried balls deep inside of me.

"Oh, Elsy," he says, his smile audible. "Don't ever change."

With that, he pulls back and slams home again. Arousal coils within me as he fucks me with even, measured strokes. He sets one hand on my upper back, applying steady pressure until I drop onto my forearms to bury my face in the pillows.

This man treats me like a queen, my pleasure his priority, but he doesn't treat me like a delicate flower. Or like I'll break. No, he treats me like his equal.

Because I am. Just because he's a millionaire hockey player doesn't mean he's better than me or that he's more important than I am. We're the same, he and I. We're just people—people who have anxiety, people who have fought from the brink of panic, people who have loved and lost and learned.

And as Wyatt fucks me, his hands touching every part of me, I know it goes beyond the physicality. He's touching my soul, too. He's touching my heart.

He loves me. And one day, probably very soon, I'm going to tell him I love him, too. I'm halfway there already.

It's taking me longer to get there, but it's not a race. It's a journey—one we get to go on together. And there's no finish line, there's no end to this. Until the day we both decide to call it quits, I'm in this—for as long as he'll have me.

To have and to hold, from this day forward.

Wyatt's hand smacks my ass, jolting me back to the present moment.

"You with me, Els?" His voice is gruff, as rough as gravel.

"Hold me." My words are soft, hardly more than a whimper, but when he drapes his body over mine and brackets me in, I lean my head back on his shoulder.

"Anytime," he says, his arm curling around my belly.

His pace slows, no longer frantic as he fucks into me.

And as the fire inside of me climbs higher and higher, as he holds me and murmurs into my ear, I know that this is it— this is what I've been looking for all these years. I've been so tripped up over our past, I never let myself consider a future.

It's what I want. Him and me. Me and him.

Forever.

My orgasm hits before I'm ready for it, my whole body alight with pleasure. Wyatt fucks me through it, and only when I collapse onto the bed does he seek his own release.

With a shout, he tenses as his cock jerks inside me, spilling into the condom. He pulls out of me and collapses onto the bed. Immediately, he pulls me into his arms, and I set my head on his chest, directly over his pounding heart.

"I love you," he murmurs, pressing a kiss to my hair.

"Love you, too," I finally get the courage to say back.

And then I black out.

thirty

. . .

Wyatt

I THOUGHT I knew what love was. I thought I was happy. Turns out there's nothing better than waking up beside the woman I love, naked and sated, with her knowing exactly how I feel about her.

Well, there might be one thing better. But I don't think either of us is ready for me to put a ring on her finger. Soon. Probably sooner than I expect.

Since I've been spending my time at Elsy's, the fridge is pretty bare, so I order delivery from the diner across the street. The doorman brings it up right as I'm getting out of the shower. Elsy's still asleep as I arrange our omelets, toast, and fruit onto two plates. She's not usually a big breakfast person, but I know she has a full day capped off by a performance tonight. She needs to keep her strength up.

Because now that I've had a taste of her, I won't be able to live without her. Not again.

The team's group chat is loud this morning, my phone going off every five seconds with yet another chirp from the guys. But I don't care. They can mock me all they want; I love her, and I don't fucking care who knows it.

Elsy pads into the living room shortly after nine, wearing

my shirt from last night. Her hair is adorably rumpled and her face is creased with last night's makeup.

"Good morning." Smiling broadly, I rise from the couch and meet her halfway.

"Mm. Morning." She wraps her arms around my torso, burying her face in my chest. "I slept in."

"You did." I kiss the top of her head. "You needed it."

She tilts her face up and I kiss her properly.

"How about you?"

"Good. I sleep better when you're next to me." Shaking my head, I tease, "If only I could bring you on the road with me."

She laughs. "Yeah, that's not going to happen."

"I know. I was thinking, though…"

Her eyebrows go up. "Hmm?"

"I'm playing in Boston in December, with an extra day on the ground before. It's the middle of the week, so you'd have to miss rehearsal. But you don't have any performances those days. Do you want to come? You could see Bex and everyone…"

Elsy's eyes widen. "You want me to go?"

"I thought you might like to see your friends. I know there's rehearsal to consider, but…"

"I'll make it happen," she states.

Kissing her, I squeeze her shoulders. "Good. So it's a date. I'll see if I can get you on the team plane, otherwise I'll book tickets for you."

"You don't have to do that," she says, puffing up with indignation. "I can—"

"I want to."

All the fight seeps out of her.

"Elsy, I want to do this for you. Will you let me?"

She swallows, then nods. "Thank you."

"Anytime." Tightening my arms around her, I drop a kiss on her forehead. "Come, eat. Your breakfast is getting cold."

"You cooked?" She sounds skeptical, and rightfully so.

"There's a cute place across the street. I'll take you next time."

"You think there will be a next time?" A smile teases her lips as she takes her seat.

"Now that I've had you in my bed, you'll be lucky if I let you go."

She giggles. "Yeah, good luck with that. I can be pretty slippery."

A bolt of heat shoots through me, remembering exactly how slick she gets. "Oh, trust me. I've got a handle on you."

Triumphant, she digs into her breakfast. "It's cute you think that."

———

After breakfast, I drive her home to get ready for her day and then head to the practice facility. It took a few weeks, but now I finally feel like I'm part of the team, like I belong here. This is my team now.

That doesn't mean my life is suddenly perfect, though. My panic attack has been weighing heavily on my mind. I thought I'd worked through all of my self-doubt when it comes to my family, but it's clear there's still a long way to go. The appointment with my therapist the other day only reminded me I still have to do the work; I can't bury it and pretend it doesn't exist.

I need to tackle this head-on. Even if I can't get past this lingering worry. I'll never be good enough for them; I know I never will be.

But that doesn't mean other people feel the same way about me. Elsy doesn't think the way they do; she's choosing to be part of my life. My sister and I have never been closer. And then my new teammates... they're my family now.

I don't want to do this. But I know I probably should.

Pulling out my phone, I exhale to the count of four, and then click on the contact.

The line connects on the third ring.

"Hi, Mom." Can she hear the way my voice shakes?

"Wyatt?" Confusion laces her tone. "Why are you calling me?"

Because I don't. My teammates might call their moms daily, but I probably only call home once every few weeks. It's my sister I talk to much more often.

"Just wanted to say hi." I hold my breath.

"Hello?" She gives an awkward laugh. "How are things? Bex said she visited you."

"Yeah. She came for the weekend."

That was nearly a month ago. It's been that long since I called home. And it's not like she's called me in the time since. It's always me reaching out.

"How nice."

A stilted silence stretches between us.

"I'm dating someone," I blurt out.

"Oh. Okay?"

I've never brought a girlfriend home, not since high school.

"I'm dating someone and it's serious," I continue. Running my palms over my pants, I exhale again, focusing on my breathing. "I love her. She might be the one. And I just… I wanted you to know."

"That's great, Wyatt." There's a warmth in my mother's voice that wasn't there before. "What's her name? Can we meet her?"

"Her name is Elsy. She's friends with Bex. You met her at the Stanford graduation."

"Oh." I can tell she doesn't know how to take that. "And your sister is okay with this?"

"She's happy for us," I say firmly. "I was thinking…

maybe you and Dad could come to Austin for a weekend? You can meet her again. Properly, this time."

"Oh, I don't know…"

She can't even pretend to be enthusiastic. My heart breaks. Why is it that nothing I do is ever good enough?

"I'll send you the tickets, and I can handle all the arrangements." My voice cracks and I clear my throat. Why can't they at least pretend to be interested in me? "I want you to get to know her."

"It's serious?" Mom asks.

She's not listening to me; I just told her it was.

"As soon as she's ready, I'm going to ask her to marry me."

When it's time, I won't ask for my grandmother's ring, even though it's been passed down through the family for three generations. I'll buy her a new one—without strings and ugly memories attached.

"Wow."

I absolutely hate this. Why do I keep putting myself through this torture, trying to make my parents love me when they clearly don't care? Why do I keep reaching out, knowing they will rebuff me at every turn?

No more. I can't put myself through this anymore. It hurts too much.

I have to let them go.

"Let me know what weekend will be good for you to visit."

I'm putting the ball in their court. If they don't give me a date, I won't book the tickets. If they don't put in at least a modicum of effort, I'm dropping the rope. They can figure it out.

When I have kids, *if* Elsy and I have kids, they likely won't know their grandparents. And although part of me is sad about that, another part of me is relieved. I don't have to keep killing myself, forcing a relationship they clearly don't want. I don't have to keep putting myself out there for people who won't do the same in return.

My mom is quiet on the other end of the line, though I can hear her breathing, so she hasn't hung up. She's just not saying anything.

She never says anything.

I swallow the lump in my throat, my eyes stinging.

This is it. I have to let them go.

"Listen, I've got to run, I have to get on the ice soon." I'm not even dressed for practice yet, but she doesn't need to know that. "I'll talk to you later."

"Bye, Wyatt."

She doesn't say she loves me, like my teammates' moms tell them. She doesn't say she hopes to see me soon.

She just says goodbye.

And maybe that's the sign I was looking for all this time. I'm never going to be enough for them. I'm never going to be the child they're proud of.

I don't resent Bex for being their pride and joy. She doesn't crave their approval the same way I do. She's never held it against me for being dragged to all my practices and tournaments growing up. She doesn't care that I dropped out of school to play hockey for a living.

She just wants me to be happy.

My sister loves me unconditionally, and I've never doubted that for a second. Instead of wondering why my parents can't do the same, I need to live my life for *me*, not for them.

Blowing out a breath, I email my therapist. It's clear I've got some work to do. I'm finally ready to get started.

thirty-one

. . .

Elsy

WHEN I PUT out the call on social media for new friends, I wasn't sure what to expect. A bunch of people replied to my post and we've been messaging back and forth since.

But who am I to organize something like this?

There are seventeen people in the back room of this café. Mostly women, though there are a few guys and two people who introduced themselves as nonbinary.

Cis, het, queer, trans… I'm looking for friends, and I don't discriminate. They're all welcome, as far as I'm concerned.

What's more important is who they are inside. They like romance novels and they like hockey; anything else we have in common is a bonus.

A blond woman approaches, a coffee cup in her hand. I blink when I recognize Katrina O'Connor—Anastasia's wife.

"Room for one more?" she asks, a smile curving her lips.

"The more, the merrier," one of the other women says.

My heart nearly bursts with happiness. This is exactly the inclusive environment I'm trying to foster.

Katrina bumps my arm with hers. "I didn't know you'd be here."

"I didn't know you liked hockey," I counter.

She shrugs. "I talked to some players that night at the gala. I like your boyfriend. He's cute."

My face flushes. "He wasn't my boyfriend back then."

"But he is now?" She grins at me. "Girl, he's so in love with you."

"Yeah, he is." I bury my face in my hands. "He told me last night."

One of the other women overhears. I think her name is Chloe.

"Your boyfriend told you he loves you last night?"

When I nod, my face flaming, she lets out a squeal of delight.

"He's a real-life book boyfriend," Katrina chimes in. "Super cute, totally devoted to her, and even better, he has single friends."

A murmur goes through the group, and I laugh.

"OMG!" Another person gasps. I'm fairly certain their name is Alex. I should have brought name tags. "I recognize you! You're Wyatt Whitney's partner."

Hesitantly, I nod. I don't want to be known as his possession. I want to be my own person.

"He gave an interview last night after that scene with his jersey," they continue. "He talked about your job with the symphony and the new fundraising campaign they're doing for youth music programs. It's clear how much it matters to him."

I blink. I only mentioned the program in passing. I didn't realize he was paying attention.

"He said that?"

They nod. "It was super motivating. I pledged a donation. It's nice to see a hockey player care about the arts."

"It is," I murmur, my head spinning.

Wyatt has never made me doubt his feelings for me. He's

never played games. He's apologized profusely for what happened thirteen years ago.

When we're together, I'm *happy*. He makes me so freaking happy. I enjoy being around him to the point I'd rather spend time with him watching paint dry rather than be by myself. And as someone who needs a lot of alone time to recharge, that's *huge*.

I think… I think I love him.

I played it off last night at the pub as a joke. I wasn't ready to think it through, especially not with everyone watching.

But now…

Coming home to him is the best part of my day, second only to waking up beside him. When he's on a road trip, I count down the hours until I can see him again. And not in an obsessive, can't survive without him, codependent kind of way.

More like… I can survive perfectly fine without him, but it would be a half-life. It would be a slog to get through each day. The world is tinged in shades of gray, but when he's around, everything is in bright technicolor.

He makes my life brighter. He makes everything better.

I don't want to live without him, not for a single minute more.

"Oh, *fuck*," I whisper. I have a vague memory of saying it last night, but I can't remember if that was a dream.

Katrina looks at me with worry. "What's wrong, sweets?"

"I love him." I stare at her, not really seeing her. "I really love him."

"You have to tell him," Chloe insists.

Half rising out of my seat, I start to gather my things, until Katrina pulls me down.

"But not right now," she says. "We're being social and making friends. You can tell him when he gets home tonight."

With a laugh, I settle back in my chair, turning my attention to the people around me.

"How do you feel about a romance-only book club?" I ask, and I'm surprised when people agree and want to make plans.

This will be good for me. I wanted a fresh start, a blank slate. I'm finally getting what I wanted—and it feels *good*.

The group decides on another date to meet up and a book to discuss. It's a title I've read before, a book I thoroughly enjoyed. The discussion is sure to be a good one.

Maybe eventually, I'll be comfortable inviting people into my life for real. I've missed grabbing dinner with friends or having them over for a movie night. I've missed socializing for fun and not for networking or charming patrons. I've missed feeling like *me*.

Katrina squeezes my arm before she heads off, and as I drive across town to the rehearsal studio, there's a lightness in my chest. I hadn't noticed how heavy that weight was until it was lifted off.

Anastasia is already in her chair by the time I arrive.

"I just had coffee with your partner," I tell her as I take out my violin.

"Oh?" She doesn't seem surprised. "Katrina mentioned she was going to a meetup."

"It was good to see her. Maybe…" I swallow my fear. I can do this. "Maybe we can go for dinner. The four of us."

My colleague smiles. "So things are going well with the hockey player?"

Dipping my head, I can't hide my smile at the thought of Wyatt Whitney and his stupid, gorgeous face. He makes me so freaking happy. How did I think, even for a minute, I wasn't in love with him?

"Really well."

"In that case, we'd love to," Anastasia says. "We can work out a date after rehearsal."

The conductor leads us through the warm-ups and then the pieces on our docket. The session is smooth, although a tuba player has some difficulty. Not the tuba player who was asked to leave the symphony a few weeks ago—it was his replacement.

I'm finally part of the group for real. After rehearsal, two of the clarinetists and a flutist invite Anastasia and me for dinner before our performance, along with one of the French horns and a saxophonist.

It's a lighthearted group that gathers at the Italian restaurant two blocks away from the studio. I've had conversations with most of the gang over the last few weeks. They've all been excessively welcoming.

I might have doubted it before, but I'm certain now this is where I'm meant to be.

After our performance, I'm riding an adrenaline high like none other. Wyatt went to O'Malley's with the guys but heads home at the same time I do, meeting me in the garage under my apartment.

He kisses me like it's been thirteen years since he last saw me, not thirteen hours. I burrow into him, drawing as much comfort as I can.

When he pulls back, he takes my hand in his and leads me to the elevator bank.

"How was the performance? Everything went well?"

"It was great." My words come out awkward, cold. Forced.

Wyatt hums as we ride up to the apartment. Once we're inside, shoes kicked off, he turns to me.

"What's wrong?"

"Nothing's wrong. Why would you think something is wrong?" My voice rises into a squeak.

He points at me. "Something's freaking you out. Is it something I said? Am I too much?"

My heart breaks at the pain on his face. He thinks he did something wrong, but he did everything exactly right. He's perfect.

"I—" The words get stuck.

"Whatever it is, we can talk through it. We can fix it," he says, taking my hand. "Just talk to me."

"I lied."

Slowly, he blinks at me. "You lied?"

"I lied. When you told me you loved me…"

His face draws into a frown. "I don't think I want to hear this."

"I'm saying this all wrong." I scrub a hand over my face. "Wyatt, I think I'm falling in love with you. And that absolutely fucking terrifies me, but—"

Joy spreads over his face. "You love me?"

Swallowing my fear, I nod. "I love you." And when the world doesn't crash around us, I laugh. "I love you."

He lets out a whoop of delight, pulling me into his arms and crushing me into him.

"I love you so fucking much," he says into my ear, holding me so close I can feel the steady pulse of his heartbeat against mine.

"I love you more," I tease, loving the way his eyes flash with happiness.

"I talked to my mom today," he says.

"Oh?" He doesn't mention his parents often, but I know he thinks about them. It weighs heavily on him they aren't closer. It doesn't bother me that I'm not close to mine; it's better for all of us that way. I've got Mitch and Bex and, now, Wyatt. That's all I need.

"I invited them to come to Austin, to meet you."

Blinking back my surprise, I tell him, "I'd love to meet your parents."

He shrugs. "Yeah, well, you might not get a chance. She wasn't enthusiastic."

My heart breaks all over again. "Wyatt…"

"But it's okay," he says. "I can't be the only one trying. If they don't want to have a close relationship, that's their right. I can't force them to love me."

"They do. In their own way, they do." I lay my hand on his cheek. "And I'll be there to support you, every step of the way."

"I know. I haven't doubted that." His stormy blue eyes meet mine. "I'm ready to start my own family."

I freeze. "Your own family?"

We've talked about kids in the abstract in that we both want them, but…

"Yeah. You and Bex. Mitchell, too, I guess, since it seems like we're stuck with him." He gives me a wry smile. "You adopted Henry as your brother, so I guess he's part of the family. Anyone else you want to include?"

"Our own family…"

"We can pick and choose the people we spend our energy on," Wyatt says. "We don't have to subject ourselves to people who don't value us. Who don't care about the ways they hurt us." His sharp inhalation makes my heart race. "I want to surround myself with the people who care about me, not the people who don't."

"I think that's a wonderful idea," I drawl. "And… the other type of family?"

"As soon as you're ready, we can try for some kids. Teach them how to skate and how to play the violin." A slow grin spreads over his face. "But let's get married first."

I laugh. "First you want to start a family, now you want to get married?"

"When we're ready," he amends. "I know without a doubt I want to spend the rest of my life with you. You're it for me. You're my person."

My breath catches. Is he saying what I think he's saying?

"We don't need to rush," he continues. "As soon as we're both ready, we can get married. I just want you to know where my head's at. I want to build a life with you. However long it takes, whatever the timeline, I want my future to be with you."

I curl into him. "I want that, too."

Wyatt kisses me. "Then it's a plan. You and me, together. Forever."

epilogue

. . .

Elsy

WHEN WYATT SUGGESTED we go on a vacation to celebrate the end of the season, I thought it would be low-key. Casual. Not... this. A five-star resort in the Caribbean is not something I ever envisioned for myself.

"Surprise!" A group of hockey players jump out at us.

With a startled laugh, I take in our friends. Henry, Puppy, and Viggy are here, plus a few other guys from the Aces. There are players from Wyatt's tenure with Philly, including those who have gone on to other teams. And then there are a few players from the Grizzlies...

Vanessa waves at me from under Sven's arm, and Rachel and Jake grin. I even recognize Seb Henry and his fiancée, Audrey. Bex is standing with them, and she walks forward, grabbing me in a hug.

"Congratulations," she says in my ear. "I'm so happy for you two."

"Thank you."

The weight of his ring on my finger is one I'm slowly getting used to.

"Hey," I say, nudging her. "This makes you my sister."

"Finally!" Bex tosses up her hands. "I've only wanted a sister forever." She hugs me close. "I'm so glad it's you."

"Did you know he was going to propose?"

I kind of thought he'd do it on this trip, but he surprised me by popping the question two weeks ago. We went for a walk at Lady Bird Lake and then for lunch at the deli across from my old apartment, now that I'm officially all moved into his condo. Over tuna salad croissants and club sandwiches, as he was handing over his pickle spear, he asked me to marry him.

Of course, I said yes. And not just for a lifetime of pickles.

"I had a hunch." She winks at me. "He showed me a few pictures from the store, but he's the one who picked it." She plucks my hand into hers, admiring the ring. "It's gorgeous."

When it comes to jewelry, I'm a minimalist. The simple white-gold band with a single oval diamond is perfect for me. If I could have imagined a dream ring, it's exactly what I would have asked for.

He knows me, sometimes even better than I know myself.

Henry steps forward, nudging Bex away, and I let him wrap me in a hug. "So happy for you, honey," he murmurs into my ear. "He doesn't treat you right, you let me know, and I'll remind him what he stands to lose."

I grin. "Thanks. I don't think we'll need to, though."

Wyatt is across the resort restaurant, chatting with a few of the other guys. His broad smile is relaxed, no hint of anxiety. Neither of us will ever be "cured" of the insidious thoughts that plague our brains. But with medical management, regular therapy—both separate and together—and a lot of work, we can live happy, fulfilling lives.

"So how do you like your engagement party?" Henry asks.

"Oh? Is that what this is?"

"Of sorts. What could be better than a week in tropical paradise with all of your best friends?"

I look around the room. There's one person conspicuously missing…

"Where's Mitch?" I ask. I can't believe he would miss something like this, even with everything that's been going on.

He laughs. "His flight is delayed. He'll be here soon," he promises. "He texted me the details. Whitney had me coordinating everything."

"Really? You?"

"Don't sound so surprised." Henry laughs. I poke him in the side and he twitches. "The plan was to propose last night, but he jumped the gun. He couldn't wait. You think it's hard to wrangle cats, try twenty hockey players *and* a secret proposal."

"I'm glad you did." I squeeze him around the waist. "You're the best."

"Anything for you two." He gives me a small smile. "I meant it when I said you're my sister now. You're stuck with me."

"I wouldn't have it any other way."

Pulling me across the room, he introduces me to his brother, Sebastian, and Seb's fiancée, Audrey, the daughter of Boston's coach. We've met socially a few times while I was still living there, but we don't know each other well. I guess that's going to change now that Henry's adopted me.

As I mingle with friends both old and new, my eyes keep drifting across the room. Wyatt is so happy. I understand what he meant now about making our own family. We discarded the people who dragged us down, the people who didn't want the best for us. And now we're embarking on a new life together, surrounded by the people who matter most.

Dinner is delicious and followed by drinks, then dancing, and it's close to two o'clock in the morning when the party finally dies down.

Luckily, we have the better part of a week to party. But first, time for bed.

Bex has a cabin close to ours. Wyatt is between us as we stroll to the beachfront bungalows. The steadiness I feel when his hand is in mine hasn't gone away. If anything, I feel even more secure. His other arm is around his sister's shoulders as they argue playfully about which Teenage Mutant Ninja Turtle the other is.

The only thing that could make tonight better would be—

My best friend steps around the corner, and I grin, racing toward him.

"Mitch!" I practically leap into his arms and he catches me like I weigh nothing, even though that's decidedly not the case.

"Hey, Els." He cups the back of my hair as he hugs me. "You look good. Happy. Congratulations."

"Thanks. I am. I really am." Taking in his haggard appearance, I run my hand through his hair. "You don't."

He sighs. "It's been a long couple of weeks."

His team was bounced out of the first round of playoffs. Austin made it to the second round before crumbling.

Mitch's eyes flicker behind me, widening. He clears his throat and shuffles me under his arm so he can shake Wyatt's hand.

"Good to see you, man."

My *fiancé* grins at him. "You, too." He pulls him in for a bro hug.

Mitch's face scrunches in confusion. His eyes flick from me to Bex and then back to Wyatt, narrowing.

"Have you met my sister?" Wyatt says. "This is Bex. B, this is Mitchell."

All the color drains from Mitch's face. "Fuck."

Bex glares at him. "You look like a Nick to me."

———

Want more Elsy and Wyatt? Check out the extended epilogue five years later here.

How do Bex and Nick know each other? Find out more in *Game Misconduct*!

afterword

Thank you for reading *Tripped Up*. This book is my baby and I absolutely love it to pieces.

Reviews are more important than readers realize. If you liked this book, please leave me a review!

Join my newsletter to stay in the loop! Lots of unfunny quips, unsuccessful attempts at wit, and general grouching about the writing process.

xoxo,

Allie

what's next?

Thank you for reading *Tripped Up*.

For more neurodivergent love stories, check out *The Thought of You*, where Johanna discovers she's autistic when her reformed playboy roommate tells her.

In your hockey era? Check out *Puck Me Twice*, featuring Vanessa and the autistic hockey player she asks to be her fake boyfriend, not knowing he wants it to be real.

about the author

Allie is a queer and AuDHD writer with a hyper-fixation on inclusivity and representation. She loves the color purple, Michigan football, the Detroit Lions, and the Boston Bruins. When she's not absorbed by a book, she likes to spend time with her nephews.

A San Diego, CA native now residing in South Carolina, she is allergic to the cold, rain, snow, and mosquitos.